Murder at St. Katherine's

A Phoenix Detective Mystery
Book #2

Shelly Young Bell

To Bonnie and Rose

For Your Inspiration and Encouragement

This is a work of fiction. It is not biographical nor autobiographical. All names, characters, places, and incidents are the product of the author's imagination or are used fictitiously, and any resemblance to actual persons living or dead, places or events is entirely coincidental.

The Phoenix Detective Mysteries
A Very Sisterly Murder, Book 1
Murder at St. Katherine's, Book 2
The Diamond Dunes Murders, Book 3
The Cabot College Murders, Book 4
Population 10, The Dead End Murders, Book 5
R.S.V.P. to Murder, Book 6
Murder on the Promenade Deck, Book 7
Murder at 13 Curves, Book 8

Historic Novel
Stand Like the Brave

Copyright © 2019 Shelly Young Bell
Revised / Updated 2022
All Rights Reserved
ISBN-13: 9781080341252

A flubbed robbery investigation has left Detective Ann Essex in rehab with a broken hip. Detective William Dancer is on desk duty, with not much to do these last few days before Christmas but work out, write, bake cookies, and try to decide on his future career path. A trip north to Buckelsmere from Philadelphia will involve Bill and Ann once again in a little holiday murder, this time a little too close to home.

Follow Detective Ann Essex, her associates Detectives Bill Dancer and Tom Van Pelt, best friends Suzanne and Che-Che, and investigative daughter Robin and her ever present friend Caela, as they solve murders and piece together the mysteries they encounter.

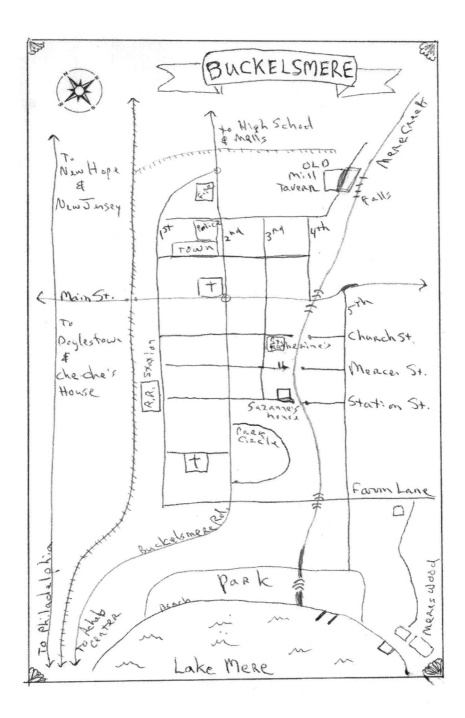

Chapter 1

December 17

Detective Bill Dancer stood behind a rusted metal fire escape against the frozen brick wall, hoping his camel hair coat was far enough away from the wall to avoid any contamination with garbage, urine and God knew what else. He waited along with the others participating in the stakeout. As he did, his mind wandered back and forth between the stakeout, the wisdom of his decision of police work as a profession, and the correct usage of the words lie, lay, lain, laid. Bill decided that given they had been unsuccessful these last six weeks catching the jewelry store robbers in the cold December evenings, he'd perhaps be much better off at home in his studio apartment, writing.

Detective Ann Essex, knelt behind some trash cans in the same alley waiting for something, anything to develop. This case had finally come to a head when Bill's legwork had allowed them to identify the store that would be next, Lou Simon's Diamonds. And it might be tonight. Ann had been huddled in the cold and dark alley for a couple of hours now, along with her associate, Detective Bill Dancer, and a team of armed and ready police officers. The Philadelphia Police Detectives in the 6th District, the

Central Division, didn't think they needed a S.W.A.T. team, since the robbers had not actually fired their guns during their robberies, but armed officers were included. Knowing where and approximately when they would probably strike next had been a big help. The neighborhood was totally spooked by the now anticipated weekly robberies. Which store would be next? How should they fend them off? And so, Ann, Bill and the rest of the detail waited in the dark and the cold.

Plain clothes police lookouts loitered at each corner in every direction of Lou Simon's Diamonds, posing as normal citizens. At the first sign of the robbers approaching, everyone would be alerted by a cell phone message and then the action would start.

This particular band of robbers had hit six jewelry stores in the past six weeks, but hadn't left any other clues to help the police decide which store might be next, if any. At some point, the robbers would probably stop on their own, or provoke some store owner into taking the law into his own hands and solving the problem himself. Permanently. But who else would be a casualty in that situation? Ann knew that scenario often did not end well.

Ann smiled as she thought about how her young associate detective, Bill, had decided to investigate the customers of the stores having been hit. When these lists were compared to each other, Bill noticed that one customer had visited all six stores within the few days before that store had been robbed. This man always purchased a pair of sterling silver hoop earrings as a Christmas gift for a girlfriend. Same man, same purchase, same story. All six stores confirmed it, but the man had paid in cash as the purchase wasn't very expensive, so the police didn't have a paper trail to follow.

Bill had taken this information plus several very grainy photos from CCTV cameras on the street and handed them around to all the other stores in the Jewelry Row area. He instructed each store owner to show it to their clerks, study it and be ready for this man buying silver hoop earrings. It was the tell. If they encountered this man, their store was next, and the police would be ready.

Ann and Bill tried hard to hide their gratification that Bill's legwork had paid off. A clerk at Lou Simon's Diamonds confirmed he had sold a pair of sterling silver hoop earrings to the man in the photo. It was hard for Ann and Bill to keep from smiling all afternoon in advance of starting the stakeout. Ann had known it might take several days before they had any outcome, but they had to be ready each night leading up to the night the robbers appeared. If it all worked out, an arrest would be made this time around. Hopefully this evening, then they could spend the Christmas holidays at home with their families, a job well done. Fingers crossed.

To pass the time, Ann once again went over what they knew about this spate of robberies. They had all taken place just as the store was about to close for the day – so the exact time varied depending on the store and day of the week. Since the robbers had sent a man into the store in advance to the actual robbery that same week, he was easily recognized as a previous cash-paying customer by the store staff and welcomed in, even though they were just locking up for the night. But this time, this man would have brought two friends who came in quickly right behind him, pulling up their masks from around their necks, and withdrawing handguns as soon as the door was locked behind them. What were these store owners and clerks to do? Life and limb were more important than the money in the till and a handful of diamond rings, which of course were insured and could be replaced. Under the threat of being shot, the clerks always readily handed over the cash they had at hand, and unlocked any jewelry display cases the men with guns pointed out. The robbers quickly bagged it up and put it into an inconspicuous plastic grocery shopping tote. While the leader watched at the door, the other two would make the employees lay on the floor, bind their hands and feet, stuff a handkerchief into their mouths, and quietly exit the store. In and out in less than five minutes. Once out the door, the three would walk away in three different directions and remain unseen until the next time.

Ann's normal informant for jewelry fencing had not been contacted by this particular group, so Ann figured that these robbers were from out of town, coming into Philadelphia to do the reconnaissance and then the actual robbery. The jewelry was then either transported far enough away before being fenced so it was not recognized as hot, or had been stashed for the future – wait a few years, then fence it when no one was still looking for those particular items.

Luckily when Bill showed the photos of the suspected robber to the sales team at Lou Simon's Diamonds, they agreed pretty quickly that yes, that man had come into their store. He had purchased a pair of inexpensive silver hoop earrings for his lady friend with a wink and the comment he might be back for something 'more expensive'. They were marked as the next store to be hit.

And so, every night since, Ann, Bill and a squad had camped out here in the alley, on the street and in the store, waiting until after closing time. As it was mid-December, the stores were staying open later now for the Christmas rush, making their wait longer than normal. Stakeouts were never fun. Usually boring. Usually not even productive. This one, crowded behind trash cans for hours, in the December cold and wind had definitely not been fun. And this night, an icy mist had developed in the air, making the wait even more miserable. Ann tried not to think about her commute home later to the far northern suburb of Buckelsmere where she and husband John and daughter Robin had moved at the end of the last school year. She hoped the roads remained clear of ice. As one drove north out of the city, the temperature would drop a few degrees and the worse the driving conditions would become. Focus, she told herself, focus on right now, not the drive, not the exhaustion, not the stack of things left to do for Christmas – the presents, the wrapping, the decorating, the food planning. Focus!

Ann could see twinkling colored Christmas lights in the store windows, refracting though the damp air, making tiny colored starbursts on her glasses. She blinked several times trying to refocus, hoping it was the mist on her glasses and not her eyes themselves tonight that seemed to make it difficult to see. A few cars drove slowly by, looking for that elusive parking spot. She wanted to look at her phone to see what time it was, but any movement, or show of light might be at the most inopportune moment and the robbers might see it, alerting them to the presence of the police. The feeling that it had to be getting close to closing time made her heart beat a little faster. If it was going to be tonight, it would be any minute. Ann didn't normally help out on the actual stakeouts, but had offered to do tonight's so a young colleague could attend his son's school holiday concert.

Ann heard Bill slowly pull up his coat sleeve and look at his watch. He, too, must sense the time. Her phone vibrated in her hand. The signal. Someone had spotted the threesome approaching. Then, as three men came into view, Ann blinked a few more times to clear her eyes, straightened her glasses, and watched as the three robbers walked unhurriedly, silently to the store's front door. Here they paused, took a quick look around, and seeing a young clerk approach the front door to lock it for the night, grabbed the doorknob first and entered the store.

The plan was to wait three minutes or so, then quietly position themselves where they would nab the robbers as they exited the store, and take them quietly. That was the plan.

However, plans often do not go as one would wish. An older woman came down the sidewalk in the direction of the store walking a dog, and would not be hurried out of the way quickly enough when approached by one of the plain clothes policemen. She started to throw a fuss, thinking she was being accosted on the street. Ann heard Bill whisper "Oh, no!" to himself. It could only mean the robbers were now aware of the police stakeout – that they had probably looked outside to see what the commotion on the street was, and had decided that they were not coming out as was their normal pattern.

Ann stood up, and she and Bill moved out into the street. The three robbers burst out of the store unexpectedly upon seeing them, and ran in three different directions with great speed and determination to escape capture. Well, obviously it was going to be Plan B tonight.

There was a crack, a sudden burst of sound in the icy air, a quick white flash as a shot rang out. Ann couldn't tell who was firing, but usually if one side fired their guns, both sides fired their guns. It was too late to duck back into the alley, Ann decided her best option was to get low behind a parked car, so she turned and took a few quick steps towards a black Lexus. She hadn't realized that the silver icy mist had frozen to every surface by that point, and her shoes were not up to the to task – she missed her footing, twisted the whole way around and fell heavily into the street. After the initial shock of realizing that she was on the ground, she knew she should stay down, just in case. And then there was shouting, a couple more shots and a great deal of confusion and pain.

Ann couldn't see. She'd lost her glasses in the fall. She wanted to find them, but realized she couldn't move her right side. She could not get back up on her feet. This is not good, Ann said to herself. Things happened so very fast from then on. A swarm of men in blue as well as the plain clothes officers descended upon the three robbers, chasing after them. But Ann knew the robbers had the advantage. They probably had an escape route, and the police could only chase and hope to apprehend them as their original plan had fallen apart.

Bill turned back around to speak to Ann. In horror, fear rising from his heart to his throat, he saw she was on the ground. His policeman's fear of having a fellow officer hurt coursed through him. "Officer down!" he yelled, holstering his gun and running to her. Kneeling, ignoring the grime and wetness rising through his expensive wool pants, he quickly tried to assess what was wrong, where she'd been shot, asking himself how could this have happened!

"No, no, I'm not hit. I don't think so anyway. I slipped on the ice and fell, but I can't move my right side, or my right leg," Ann said to him, grasping his offered arm, as he held her head and shoulders off the cold wet pavement.

At that point, it started to sleet pretty hard, proving that yes, things can always get worse. Sharp needles of ice stung Ann's face. Tired, in pain, frustrated, Ann knew she had to show a toughness she wasn't feeling for the sake of Bill and the other members of the squad right now. She let Bill hold her, protecting her from the increasingly annoying sleet. His arms were strong, his voice reassuring, but she could hear an edge to it that she had not noticed before. Here was a Bill Dancer that Ann did not know, a Bill Dancer letting his inner feelings and compassion surface and control the moment. They had shaken hands once, only once – on the Monday she hired him as her associate detective and heir apparent. That was the only time they had touched. They shared their work, but that was about all. Since she had secrets to keep, Ann had always stayed a step away from him intentionally since that weekend when they had accidently met three years ago. But right now, here in the street, cold and getting colder, Ann let him hold her and she held onto him. The sleet now bounced up from the pavement, dancing all around Ann. Bill didn't know if it was sleet, his jagged emotions, or the icy fingers of Hell rising from below to ensnare them all – nothing seemed real to him.

It all happened in such a hurry. Flashing lights, more sirens, yelling voices from officers running up and down the streets trying to locate which way the robbers had gone. The robbers seemed to have vanished almost immediately. Finally, a young paramedic arrived to tell Bill to lay Ann back down so she and the other medics could examine her. Bill did, but he wouldn't move more than three feet away, hovering, watching, praying.

"Bill," Ann started to say.

"Ma'am?" Bill replied, his voice cracking ever so slightly over the two syllables. He never considered himself emotional, but this was something for which he had not prepared himself -- his superior officer down. He was unsure what had happened, what he could have done to prevent it. There would be questions and a review. She was obviously hurt and he wondered if she might not be going into shock, out here in the cold and wet night.

"Ma'am, just be quiet and the medics will get you over to Jefferson Hospital in two ticks," Bill said to her. "She said she twisted her ankle or something and fell, that she can't move her right side," Bill told the medics.

"Bill, make sure we get them – "

"It is all being taken care of. Don't think about it now. We'll do what we can," Bill said to her, but he wasn't hopeful of the robbers' apprehension at this point. He knew he'd have to leave and go back to the police station soon, to see what was happening with the pursuit, but he really felt he wanted to stay with Detective Essex. That is how he thought of her always – Detective Essex, not Ann, not Mrs. Essex, not the Phoenix as some joked about her at the police station. She was foremost a Detective; he figured that is what she'd want of him now. A young female officer came to his aid at that moment, encouraging him to go and do what he needed to do. She would stay with Detective Essex and the medics, and go with them to the hospital on behalf of the Police Department. Bill knew she was right, but was still torn between police duty and his personal loyalty to Detective Essex.

"Bill, go! Listen to me," Ann finally said, her eyes closed now, her teeth clenched against the rising pain. And so, he went, quickly, efficiently, the Detective Bill Dancer that his coworkers had come to know. He'd do his job, he'd do it 110%, and tonight he'd do it quickly, then he'd head to the hospital. The initial sick feeling in his stomach had changed to a cold hardness. Detective Essex was alive, not shot, but hurt nonetheless. Emotions he did not know he had, questions to which he did not know the answers, decisions that still had to be made – all were pushed aside right now in his efforts to get on with things. Bill turned and walked away to find the rest of the team and discover what was happening in the pursuit of the robbers.

Chapter 2

December 17

The waiting room at Jefferson Hospital had filled up with other police officers, press and eventually Ann's family – husband John and daughter Robin. Police Commissioner Washington, the top man, had been called immediately when it was reported that a member of the police force had been injured. He was there for public relations, but also because police officers stuck together. They had to. Their jobs were so dangerous, and things happened so quickly that police officers had to have each other's backs, physically and mentally. The Commissioner had arrived at the hospital in a motorcade of other officials from Police Headquarters at 750 Race Street at almost the same time as the ambulance that delivered Ann to the Emergency Room entrance. As a Detective, Ann was highly thought of, well respected and key to the efficient and successful functioning of the other detectives and uniformed police that she worked with. The Philadelphia Police Department would give her her due. The Commissioner might be the boss over 6300 sworn members as well as 800 civilian personnel, but he was committed to treat each one as his own partner. He had been there once himself, on the street, so he knew what it took to do the job.

Bill Dancer had been sitting in the waiting area since he was able to get away from the station. He had spoken with the lady at the reception desk explaining that he was Detective Essex's partner, so they knew he especially needed to hear any news of her condition. The receptionist could see the worry in Bill's face, and nodded her agreement to have the doctor speak to him when it was time. Detective Essex was already in surgery when he had arrived, diagnosis a broken hip, which they were going to pin and hope for a very good recovery. Apparently, she had fallen on it just right to crack it. The surgeons, confirming this earlier with John by phone, had decided that pinning it instead of replacing it at this point was the best option.

Bill rose to meet John and Robin as they arrived and guided them to his spot on a couch in a side area away from the lingering press photographers and other inquisitive eyes. John eyed the crowd and glaring lights of the press conference area. Neither he nor Robin needed to be part of that ordeal.

"Mr. Essex, I am so sorry," Bill said.

"An accident, Detective, only an accident, thank God," John answered. "She will recover and be back to torment you soon enough. You'll see." John might try for levity but Bill could see the tightness around John's eyes, and the shallowness with which the older man drew breath. He was worried and upset, and trying very hard not to show it, especially to Robin.

Robin was thirteen. She appeared to be holding up okay at the moment, but Bill did notice the redness around her eyes. She had been crying. Thirteen, tough age – not a child, not grown up. A bewildering landscape of upheaval and uncertainty.

"It shouldn't be much longer. They took her into surgery an hour ago. Can I get you something – coffee, soda?" Bill asked.

"No. No, we'll wait until we can see her, make sure she's okay, then we'll get a sandwich or something," John answered, his hand on Robin's.

They sat in silence.

In the absence of conversation between them, Bill became conscious of the sounds, sights and smells of the waiting room: the nurses talking at the desk, the automatic doors shushing open and closed, a child whining, the plastic chairs and inadequate couches, the detritus of sandwich wrappers and spent coffee cups, the antiseptic smell, the look on people's faces – patients awaiting attention, and others who had come lending a helping hand on this cold wet December evening. Bill would want to use all of these things in his writing in the future, perhaps in the crime novel he was currently working on in his spare time, what little of that there was.

Was it selfish to be thinking of his writing at a time like this? Bill stopped short of actually taking notes tonight, but he would try to remember what this was like – the emotions, the sounds and the sights – for later. For another time. Write what you know, he'd been told.

This particular night and the accident pressed the urgency of his making decisions about things he had been thinking, questioning, and putting off for a while now.

Three years in Philadelphia. Three years off the farm and the local rural police force back home. Three years working at Detective Essex's right hand. She had taught him, guided him, encouraged him to step up to a much faster paced work environment. Yet, after all this time, he felt no closer to her than that first week on the job. He respected her more as he now knew what a tough and thorough detective she was. He understood how she thought and worked. He learned how to anticipate what she might want or need professionally. But tonight, in this hospital, what did he really know about her? Why did he feel so annihilated by what had happened to her?

Bill had seen some terrible things as a city detective. It was what he originally had wanted – a higher level of crime to fight and solve. But now, he was wondering how long he would want to keep up this pace. The brutality that man could inflict on his fellow man was appalling. Good as it felt to bring these criminals to justice, and that was his job after all, it often had been difficult to leave the job at the office. Recently, there were more and more nights when he would lie awake with visions of violence and death dancing in front of his eyes. Only three years here and he was beginning to feel the urge to get out. But if he did, would he consider himself a failure, a coward? Did he just need to leave this particular job and move on, or would it be better to leave police work altogether? Would he know he'd made the right move at the right time? Bill needed to reserve some of his energy if he was to pursue his passion of writing his detective stories. This job seemed to suck him dry of all his creative energy lately. He'd had some mild success with his stories being published, but he never had enough time or energy to really give it his best effort. He could stay on here in Philly, and decide to leave after maybe another year or two. More often, he was inclined to pack it in, return home, help on the farm and write. Only write. Not face another morning rising to get to the office too early with no breakfast, to face another chase, another stakeout, another body.

And then there was his self-admitted loyalty to Detective Ann Essex, who maybe now needed him more than ever. Three years. Had he expected a closeness between them? Would it have been appropriate? Especially since she was a woman? Bill remembered that weekend three years ago which he had promised himself he would never mention to her -- the weekend her whole family had been at the same country inn, The Garnet Inn, that was its name. A man had died. Coincidence? At the time he thought so. And it *had* been ruled an accidental death. Detective Essex had never spoken of it, so neither did he, following her lead on that. The weekend had been personal family time for her, so he left the fact that he had been there as well unspoken.

They were work associates, not friends; he had thought that until tonight. Tonight was different, with the stakeout, the gunfire, the accident, the abysmal weather and her not refusing his arms or the comfort he offered. This, he realized, was admission that they had been a team all along. More than just work associates, a level of mutual affection was there, too. He had just never recognized it. It had been her quiet way with him that had fooled him, he supposed. He had not recognized her eventual acceptance of him as an outsider becoming one of them. Bill wondered if maybe he had been looking for something else all along – something more in line of what a male supervisor might have offered. No, no he decided, this is exactly how a male supervisor would have been expected to treat him – guide him, instruct him, show him how to adapt and grow. No difference.

Enlightening. Bill felt remarkably better. He felt immensely and suddenly very affectionate towards Detective Ann Essex. She had treated him exactly the way he should have been treated as a junior officer, an officer needing and accepting her guidance and professional encouragement. She had a plan; he was part of it. No, they had never gone out for cheesesteaks at Pat's or Geno's after a long shift. They didn't share stories of their weekend exploits over coffee on a Monday morning. Bill hadn't sought that from her. He hadn't sought any level of personal involvement from anyone with whom he worked – a sign perhaps he felt this was a temporary job and that he *would* move on.

Bill twisted one hand in the other. Waiting was a hard game, he was learning. At thirty-three he hadn't done much hospital waiting room duty. His parents were well. He'd had no significant others. He hadn't given anyone enough time or attention for them to achieve significant status in his life. His own fault. So, he sat alone, with someone else's family this horrible night.

He worked. He wrote. He worked out at the corner gym. He slept. He did find that he enjoyed the food scene in Philadelphia more than he had anticipated. He often stopped at a new place on the way home for a cold brew and a platter of whatever was their specialty, places he'd read about online or in the Sunday Inquirer.

He had found an adequate tailor, someone who understood his desire to always look immaculately dressed, but understated. Bill enjoyed looking impeccable each day, even though it meant taking the other police officers' jokes about it with good humor. Jealous, he told himself, they are just jealous. Bill took pride in making sure his suits were the best quality fabric, were always pressed and ready to be worn. And he looked it every morning when he arrived at the police station – a crisp starched white shirt, all buttons on and working, pressed custom suit, his hair neat and brushed back, his dimpled, boyish face cleanshaven. Disarming to many, Bill's appearance belied his quick brain and sword-sharp determination. Often, he would be written off as a dandy and nothing more. Occasionally Bill would play that card to his advantage as he could seem dim and preoccupied with his appearance, disarming those around him.

Tonight, he felt none of those things. Rather he felt old, cold, tired, worn, dirty; his emotions too bare, too exposed. He was hungry and yet wouldn't leave to satisfy that – not until the doctors had come out to tell them some news on Detective Essex.

Unconsciously, Bill picked at his fingernails, thinking. Okay, he decided, he'd get through this situation at the hospital, do whatever he could for John and Robin, get himself home, have a hot shower and a bowl of hot soup, then to bed. One small step at a time. It was the only way, he knew. Tomorrow would be better, brighter, more controlled. It had to be. Christmas was only a week away. This situation would be his reason to not go home to the farm this year for the holiday. It was a five-hour drive home so it was never a casual visit. Bill felt he'd be needed at the police station because Detective Essex would be out of commission for sure. He was her de facto right-hand-man, so he'd step up. Yes, he'd step up, and try to relish the chance for the little bit of added experience, and he'd be glad to just simplify this next week or so. Try to turn it into a positive. Maybe he'd get away for New Year's, he'd tell his mother. Bill made a mental note to be sure to UPS his family's packages to them the next morning. Hopefully they would arrive in time. His two sisters would be at his parents' house, so Bill did not feel too guilty about not going.

When the doctor finally came out, he spoke with John and Robin, explaining in simple terms it was a broken hip. They had pinned it instead of replacing it. Ann was a young enough, healthy enough candidate for that procedure. The surgeons had put a few three-inch titanium screws in place to hold the bone together while the hip mended. Bill and Police Commissioner Washington listened in at the fringe of the consultation circle. Ann would be here at Jefferson Hospital for a few days, then transferred to a rehabilitation facility for a couple weeks for further healing, and physical and occupational therapy. After that she could go home with John and Robin, but must stay off that leg for two months – no weight on it at all – and then the slower, total recovery to get off the walker, off the cane and then back on her own two feet. She probably would be cleared to return to police work in three to four months, desk work before that if she felt up to the commute once she could drive again.

Bill looked at John, who returned the look. They both knew that Ann would be beside herself with that prognosis. Home, incapacitated for two months?

"I'll see what the Department wants to do, how we can help," the Commissioner said. He was all about saying the right things and assured John that the Department would stand behind Ann during her recovery and eventual return to duty. "Right now, I better talk to the press, then all this circus will calm down and clear out." The Commission then strode across the tile floor towards the microphone set up for him, his heavy, spit-shined leather shoes squeaking on the heavily waxed floor as he went.

John stayed quiet, but Bill sensed there was something John would have liked to say to the Commissioner, but that he was holding back. Bill hoped it was just John being his normal quiet, reserved self – that there wasn't something else going on.

The doctor then took John and Robin through the swinging "NO ADMITTANCE" doors to Ann's bedside in the recovery area. Bill sat back down. He would wait for John to come back out, to offer to stay if John needed him, to take Robin to their home about an hour away in the far northern suburbs. Bill knew he should stick to his original plan of just heading home, but now he felt he'd just wait and see if there was anything he could do, although he knew he'd probably be brushed aside with a "Thank you, but no thanks" reply. He didn't know John very well, having only met him on the rare social occasion, but assumed he probably was as private a person as Detective Essex was.

Tomorrow, Bill would write the incident report, do the interviews and try to straighten out the mess of this evening's debacle. He thought he might reorganize the team if they allowed him, although it seemed unlikely that the robbers would strike again, now that they knew they had been found out. Also, Bill would do damage control on anyone wanting to put a negative twist to anything that had happened tonight.

In the morning, when he could sneak away from his desk, he'd come back with candy and a poinsettia and magazines. Magazines were always good, he knew. Maybe even the magazine that just recently had published one of his stories – would he dare share that? Bill knew he'd be reconsidering that decision in the cold, harsh light of morning. Would he share his writing with Detective Essex now, or not? Was it time to take the next step in their relationship by sharing something extremely personal? Tomorrow, he'd decide tomorrow.

Chapter 3

December 21

Day five, Ann told herself. She knew she should not be keeping count – two months off her legs was going to be a long time. Day five of sixty. Already she was feeling it would be impossible. Maybe she should look at it in blocks of time. Block 1 as the time she had already spent in the hospital. Mark that Block as "done." Block 2 would be the time spent here in Buckelsmere Rehabilitation Center. Hopefully, with diligence and work she could shorten the length of this block. Block 3 as the time at home on the walker, then Block 4 on the cane, and eventually when that was over, she'd be back to being as normal as she could be. She would only think about one Block at a time. Maybe it would help with her current feelings of depression about her confinement and her moments of anxiety over the accident, the rehab and lengthy healing that lay before her. Right now, she would concentrate on some deep breathing, decent distractions and only think about the next two weeks. Ann would worry about Blocks 3 and 4 when they happened.

She had to admit she had seen a bit of progress in the last few days. The day before John had carefully moved her from the Center City

Philadelphia hospital to the Buckelsmere Rehabilitation Center, considered by medical people to be "the place to be" if you needed that sort of care. It was just south of the village where they lived, along the west shore of Lake Mere. Mereswood, their farmhouse, was only a couple of miles to the east on the eastern shore of Lake Mere. So, it would be very convenient for John and Robin to come and visit for the duration of her rehabilitation stint.

Ann had taken an extra pain pill for the trip and gladly another one afterwards, and had settled into the room that she'd call home for two weeks. Two weeks, my eye, she said to herself. She'd do what she had to do to get out of here and home with John and Robin.

The rooms were singles at this facility, which was welcoming – no one crying, carrying on, blaring the TV night and day, with their odd family members and friends under foot. It seemed a good enough place. The food was average institutional food, but Ann found she had very little appetite anyway.

The bad news, at least in the short term, was that Christmas was now only four days away, and Ann would not be able to do any last-minute food preparation and gift wrapping. She'd miss Robin's school and church functions, and there'd be no eggnog with Grand Marnier on Christmas afternoon in front of the fireplace. One of the features of their old stone farmhouse was that each of the downstairs rooms had a working fireplace. Ann had spent six months planning to light a fire in all of them on Christmas Day. She had so looked forward to this first Christmas at their new home, entertaining her family and friends. Robin was thirteen, no longer a child with a child's expectations of Christmas. Ann had hoped it was the start of more companionable holidays, with Robin starting to be a young woman. Her current situation was NOT what she had planned. The two hundred fifty-year-old farm house would be cold and dark this year, with no familiar smells of baking cookies, roasting turkeys and mulled wine. No lit candles in the windows. No snapping and crackling fires on the hearths. No out of town family and guests coming to celebrate this first Christmas at Mereswood. John had called everyone who had planned to come for the holidays with the bad news, and asked them to consider coming in the spring when Ann ought to be back on her feet. Would John even bother filling the stockings, she wondered? Where had she put that bag of stocking stuffers? Would the Christmas Tree lights even be turned on in the evenings in her absence? Too much to think about, too depressing.

Knowing her eyesight was deteriorating, and that it signaled her eventually quitting her police detective job, John had encouraged the move from the city to quiet Buckelsmere. About an hour north of Center City Philadelphia and the police station at 235 North 11th Street where Ann was stationed, it was a small borough in the green countryside of Bucks County. Rolling hills and lots of farm fields made it quiet and idyllic in comparison to the noise and bustle of the last thirteen years living and working in Philadelphia. The village of Buckelsmere was not more than six by eight blocks, nestled on the north shore of Lake Mere. Where the village met Lake Mere, there was a town park, complete with white gazebo bandstand, war memorials, and plenty of lawn for picnics and impromptu ball games. Buckelsmere held the appeal of a pretty colonial village with old homes lining the streets, each with a decently sized lot that sported old trees and lush gardens, lovingly tended by their owners. Buckelsmere was not large, but it did have a nice Main Street and several side streets filled with shops and professional offices. On the northern edge of town, they had placed the newer school complex and sport fields, walkable from downtown if you were energetic. Also, along the northern route out of town there were a couple of modern strip malls with grocery stores, chain pharmacies, and automobile dealers. Years ago, the Town Fathers had lobbied for and secured a stop on the suburban commuter train line, which was convenient for many, even if it fed the fear that Buckelsmere would over-develop into a sprawling bedroom suburb. The borough government was careful with its zoning regulations and had kept development to a minimum for many years. This pleased the old timers, but often frustrated the younger or newer residents wishing for change and modernization. The village boasted three churches, St. Katherine's Episcopal, St. Mark's Catholic and the Buckelsmere Methodist church. Buckelsmere retained the village atmosphere that both John and Ann yearned for and hoped Robin could adapt to.

    John had been so proud of having found the old farmhouse, knowing it would suit them and that Ann would have the diversion of doing it over. Ann's good friend, Suzanne Beck, lived in Buckelsmere and had talked about it for so long, that John checked it out first when it became obvious a move out of the city was needed. They told Robin and everyone else, they were making the move because Robin was to start high school, and this school district would be better suited to her, let her flourish. But Ann and John knew it was for Ann's retirement, getting their ducks all in a row before it was actually needed. Little did they know that Ann's retirement might happen so soon after they moved in. To Ann, it was obvious. she wasn't going back. Her failing eyes, her limited mobility now, her broken nerve (and she did know it had been broken), these things would only put her coworkers in danger, and she could never do that intentionally. She would wait it out, see how things went over the next six to eight weeks, but if these feelings of panic she was experiencing at the thought of returning to work continued, she for sure would retire. But no need to discuss it with the Philadelphia Police Department just yet. She would just practice the breathing and mental focusing exercises that she had googled on her laptop that John had brought to her when the feelings of being overwhelmed and panic started to rise. Ann never considered herself weak, and if this was weakness, she was not happy about it. She would conquer whatever this was. She didn't want to bring it to anyone's attention as it would get back to the Philadelphia Police Department, setting all sorts of pre-emptory psychological evaluations and testing, then consulting and therapy for it. Nonsense! She'd just get herself over it.

Murder at St. Katherine's

The farmhouse, named Mereswood by the original owners after the mere, a shallow lake, and the heavily wooded area where the house was built, was a stucco three story typical Pennsylvania farmhouse. All white, with dark green shutters and accent paint, it set on a knoll overlooking Lake Mere. There were three front doors, the second and third having been added as the farmers added onto the original one room building over the years for a growing extended family, each one opening the room out onto the stone patio overlooking the lawn and lake. A nice feature for good weather, and entertaining. When John had toured the home, that first afternoon it was on the market, he knew that Ann would love the random width hardwood floors, the open ceiling beams in the downstairs formal rooms, that there was a fireplace in each room, and that upstairs there were six bedrooms and assorted bathrooms. Okay, a bit big for just the three of them, but John knew Ann had visions of entertaining her family and friends. And with Robin growing up, John thought there'd be plenty of room for teenage girl sleepovers and parties. The fact that the house came with a gatehouse, a boathouse, five acres of old trees, flower beds and a sloping lawn to the lake just sealed the deal for him. It would be a home they could retire to in the true sense of the word retire. If eventually he was not able to maintain it, they had enough savings to hire the needed help. And as he had anticipated, Ann fell in love with the property immediately. As she set foot inside the first room, her comment to the realtor was, "Take the sign down." Confused, the realtor asked her what she meant, and she told him, "If the toilets flush, it's sold. Take the sign down." And so, John, Ann and Robin had packed their possessions and furniture from the two-bedroom condo in Center City Philadelphia, and set out for Buckelsmere one very sunny June Saturday, never to look back.

It was time to consider that nest egg Ann had put away and not touched since she returned from Scotland thirteen years ago with infant Robin. Robin's benefactors had made sure that Ann and Robin would never want for anything, but Ann had been fearful the money would make her lazy and weak, and prove to hinder teaching Robin to work for what she needed and wanted as she grew up. Ann had put it away and tried not to think about it, knowing that someday she and Robin might need it. She supposed this was the time. She could retire without worrying about the loss of her income or worrying about Robin's eventual college bills. No one would ever ask how she was able to do it, they would just assume John had money.

Ann looked at the clock. Not yet time for another pain pill. She knew that today or tomorrow they would encourage her to switch from the opioids to just industrial strength Tylenol, but she wasn't sure how she'd manage – the hip pain was still pretty intense. It had been especially bad after the therapy session she had been given this morning – once around the hallways on the walker. Step, drag the bad leg, step, drag the bad leg. The Physical Therapy person has assured her that she had done fantastic for the first session. Ann guessed the pain was as much from the surgery and staples as from the actual bone break. She'd just have to tough it out for another hour or so. She'd have to just find something to take her mind off things until then. After all, she was the Phoenix. She smiled to herself. This time though it would be a challenge to not let the broken hip keep her down and out.

A nurse arrived with a lovely potted poinsettia arrangement. "For you, Mrs. Essex. Here's the card that came with it. Where do you want me to put it?"

"I guess over there on the windowsill," Ann answered, opening the small envelope. From the other detectives on her squad, how nice, Ann thought. If they missed her now, just wait until they found out she wasn't coming back. Ann knew she had to keep that to herself for a while yet, not even sharing that plan with Bill. No one need know until she and John had everything figured out for going forward, and that might not be for weeks, she thought.

But what about Bill Dancer, she asked herself? What could she do about Bill? Ann wished she knew what to try, to do, to suggest, but nothing immediately popped up in her mind. He could stay where he was, but she knew his initial passion for fighting the constant, dark, underbelly of crime and corruption in the city was starting to wane. Ann did wonder why, as initially he had been so keen to immerse himself in the city police culture. In the three years she had worked with him, Bill had proved to be bright, adaptive, and quietly eager, but maybe not necessarily the best fit as an inner-city detective.

Ann thought about Bill and how he had matured from the younger and definitely more naïve detective he had been when he had started working with her after that weekend in Amish country. Ann reflected on that weekend, that death, her not turning her family in – no, Bill would never know all the details. Ann had not even told John what her sisters and mother had plotted, nor about the death they had arranged. No, Bill must never know either. No one must ever know. It would be her secret that she would carry to the grave.

Ann lay back against the pillows and closed her eyes, picturing that family reunion three years ago. Mother, daughters, granddaughters. And the demise of a villain. Yes, Ann was able to admit he had been a terrible villain. She had tried these last three years to justify his death, to at least rationalize that the world was a better place without him, that Robin now was safe. At the point in the stream of logic that she arrived at 'Robin,' Ann always decided that the right thing had been done. It was finished. Ann would move on. Dr. Worthington Porter could never harm her or hers again.

Keeping it from Bill Dancer had been just a matter of making conversation about that country weekend and how they met off limits. Easy, really. Bill had been so busy those first few weeks learning the routine and trying not to make any blunders. Ann doubted if Bill ever even gave that weekend a thought at this point. Ann had kept almost all personal conversation limited to a "Have a nice weekend, see you Monday" and a casual "How about a coffee?" She knew she wouldn't slip up if she stayed away from any personal conversations with Bill.

Yes, she'd have to work out how to help Bill and his career if she decided to not go back to the Philadelphia Police Force. But not today. She would think about the details to help Bill another time, postponing that project for now.

Ann could take her meals in her room, or out in the common room, which the staff encouraged in an effort to get the patients out of their rooms so not only would staff have time to clean, but also so that the patient started thinking of themselves as a regular person, not an invalid. Transitional, Ann decided. She checked the clock on the wall again – not time for lunch either. She would have forced herself to go out there, but between the pain, the awkward seating arrangements at the tables, and Lord knows what kind of tablemates she'd end up with, Ann was not enthusiastic today. Maybe in a few days.

John would arrive soon. She hoped he remembered to bring the bag of oranges, tissue paper and ribbon she asked him for. Her Christmas oranges were a priority with her. She'd get them together and at least give them out to the nurses. Some traditions were non-negotiable for her. Giving her friends and family a Christmas orange as a remembrance of her past and of St. Nicholas was one of them. Robin would be in school until noon of the 23rd December. Then she'd have until after New Year's at home. Ann hoped she would be home before Robin did go back to school. But time would tell. Until then, it would be her, her nurses, the rehab staff, her immediate family, and whoever else was holed up here. Everyone would get a Christmas Orange, at least.

Ann stared out the window, past the red of the poinsettia, out to a brown landscape and parking lot. She didn't get a room with a view. What she did get was a hospital bed, one chair, a rolling tray, a small bedside cabinet and a hanging closet. Her memories drifted to another time, another place. A cottage in the Scottish countryside. There the bleakness had actually been the draw: the treeless landscape, the tapestry of colors of the ground covers, rocks and water, of orange and brown, green and gray, of the occasional blue sky peeking through the gray mist, a lonely primitive cottage. There she had found a purpose and a peace. Ann closed her eyes to better recall the place. The cottage. Someday she would go back to her cottage. She should. Maybe soon. Thirteen years had passed. At times it seemed like yesterday, yet at other times it was a world and an age away.

Ann must have drifted off to sleep. She saw a man standing by her bedside, a man in a robe with a hood pulled up hiding his face. He was talking to her but she could not hear his words. She awoke with a terrible jolt to the artificial light, the dry heat and antiseptic smell of her room, to a rough word and then whispering. Just a dream?

She opened her eyes, straining to hear. A dream, or a vision? Never knowing, but always accepting that she had seen something. She had seen the man, but he wasn't there. She had heard something, but it wasn't the man in the vision talking. Ann decided the sound must have come from next door or across the hall. She really didn't know the lay of the facility very well yet. She glanced at the whiteboard on the wall under the clock – happy faces and the nurses' names. Seemed she was scheduled for occupational therapy at 1:45 p.m. focusing on getting in and out of the shower and getting herself dressed, so since she'd be up and using the walker again at the point, Ann made a note to check out the situation then.

Chapter 4

December 21

Christmas was boring. At least that is what it had come to as an adult with no place to go, and not much to do. Christmas was for Children, and Suzanne Beck had no children in her life. Would she ever, she wondered? She had taken to spending Christmas with other adult friends that also had no place to go and not much to do. But Suzanne was committed to trying to make merry and contemplate the true meaning of the season. All the modern hype was only that. Hype. And if Suzanne could only hold onto that thought and ignore what the media and society say Christmas ought to be, then Suzanne knew she'd be the better for it. And a bit happier, she hoped.

She'd been planning on spending this Christmas with Ann and John. Ann was her old college roommate and they'd been able to stay friends no matter how many miles and years and other people separated them. It was good to be with people you like and who like you. This year, Suzanne had especially looked forward to Christmas at Ann's new home, considerably closer to her here in the borough of Buckelsmere. Suzanne was extremely glad John had followed up on her suggestion to check Buckelsmere out first and was able to find the perfect home for them.

Christmas was a lousy time for anyone to be in the hospital. Or rehab center, as was the case for Ann. In until New Year's, John had told Suzanne. Then Ann would go home. Suzanne knew Ann joked about how the others down at the police station called her the Phoenix. Something about always rising from whatever disaster happened. Suzanne truly hoped that this broken hip would not keep Ann down, that she'd spring from these ashes as well.

It was the 21st of December. What few preparations Suzanne was going to make for Christmas had already taken place. She knew that it would be a quiet, un-festive holiday at the Essex household now that Ann was in the Rehab Center, so she was determined to make it a bit brighter, helping to keep it merry. If she could.

Suzanne entered the rehab center, pushing in through the glass doors from the freezing cold outside to the tropical warmth inside. Why did hospitals and these places keep the temperature so warm? She started peeling off hat, gloves, scarf and coat. Stopping at the reception desk, Suzanne signed in, picked up a visitor badge and asked Ann's room number.

"112", was the polite answer with a nod down the hall to the left.

The lights were on in 112. Ann sitting in the only chair in the room. She looked older, more fragile than the early 40-ish, energetic, quick-witted woman Suzanne knew Ann to be. Illness will do that to a person, she supposed.

"Hey there," Suzanne said.

"Hey there, yourself!" Ann answered. "I don't suppose you came to spring me from this place?"

"No, John told me it would be closer to the first of the year."

"I'll go crazy! I was right in the middle of a case, and now with the holidays – argh!"

Suzanne had brought a couple of paperback books, a box of cookies from Sam's Village Bakery, and a large pink and white variegated poinsettia.

"Lovely!" Ann exclaimed, "please put it over there next to that other one on the windowsill. Maybe later you could get us some real coffee to have with these cookies. The coffee they bring me is like dishwater. They must be trying to stretch their allotment of coffee supplies. No one, not even my sainted grandmother, the thriftiest person I ever knew, would have made coffee this weak."

"I'd be glad to fetch some coffee," Suzanne said.

They talked about the accident. Normally, police detectives didn't actually chase perpetrators down an icy alley, that was left to the boys in blue, but she had and here was the result. Suzanne wondered if she heard a touch of regret in Ann's voice. She watched as Ann squinted at the book covers. It seemed like her eyes were a little worse than normal. Could be the bad artificial light. Maybe it was be the meds they had her on. Suzanne couldn't be sure.

Suzanne sat and talked for a bit about having no plans except to hang out with Ann, do what she could to help, and wait until Ann got home. Suzanne's good friend, Florencia, had asked Suzanne to join her and her family for Christmas dinner, but Suzanne couldn't work up any enthusiasm for dinner with the Reyes, making pleasant conversation but wishing it were her own family. She had become very close to Florencia, whom she called Che-Che, as they both were avid family history buffs and in the Daughters of the American Revolution. Florencia Rosita Maria Reyes, that was a mouthful. No wonder Suzanne just called her Che-Che. Ann thought Che-Che sounded like a person she would enjoy spending time with in her new Buckelsmere life. Ann knew she had an ancestor that had fought in the Revolutionary War, so maybe she'd final succumb to Suzanne's frequent requests to join them. Ann made a mental note to have Suzanne bring Che-Che around for lunch once the holidays were over and Robin was back at school. There was going to be plenty of free time to fill up then.

"What else can I do for you? I know it is a real bummer being laid up like this with the holidays coming upon us quickly now. Are John and Robin going to be okay, should I bring Christmas dinner in to them?" Suzanne asked, hoping the answer would be no to the cooking bit. Suzanne would have to scramble at this point to produce something suitable. She could always do a One-Pan Turkey Oven Roast. Not fancy, but tasty. That and cookies or a pie from the bakery might fit the bill.

"Thanks for asking. Luckily John can handle himself in the kitchen. They both have said they will just come here and eat whatever pathetic offering this place brings around. I'll just let the kitchen know how many trays to bring. They must be very used to family staying for meals as it doesn't seem to be a problem at all," Ann paused. "I hate to ask, but there is one favor you could do me."

"Anything."

"Could you pick Robin up here tomorrow afternoon about 3:00 p.m. and take her up to St. Katherine's for rehearsal for the Christmas Eve service? The youth choir has a rehearsal on the 22nd and the 23rd. I guess the choir director wants to be overly sure the kids can handle the music they have been practicing all fall. And again, on Christmas Eve? Then bring her back here each day so she can go on home with John. That would free John up to be here, help me with things, talk with the doctors or rehab people when they come around. He'd be able to run and do a few last-minute things, too. I hate to ask."

"Of course! Think nothing of it. I would be glad to do it. And it would give me something to do the next couple of days, too. Give me a purpose," Suzanne admitted more to herself than Ann. "Now, let's see about some coffee."

Suzanne wandered back out of Ann's room, looking up and down the hallway taking notice of how they had decorated the Rehab Center. Institutional. Industrial tile flooring and walls painted a gray with a white chair rail that doubled as a hand rail for the infirm. Florescent strip lighting overhead. Must be sixteen rooms on this wing. But at least they were all singles and everything did look clean and bright. Not fancy, but okay for what it was. She tried to remember from which direction she had come, which direction was back to the reception area. Suzanne chose left and walked down the hallway.

As Suzanne started down the hallway, she could hear a woman crying softly, in the room next door to Ann's. Suzanne walked slower as she passed the doorway. An old woman was hunched over on her bed, crying into her sheet, clenched in her hands. Sad. So sad. Perhaps she had been given bad news. Perhaps her family could not come for the holiday and she'd be alone. Perhaps . . . well, Suzanne was getting ahead of herself. She decided an old, weeping woman alone in a rehab center was allowed a few tears, for whatever the reason, if she so chose. Normally Suzanne, the inquisitive type would venture in and ask if she could help, but Suzanne was already on one mission to fetch coffee for Ann, and coffee it would be.

Suzanne kept walking, eventually coming to the reception area where there was a console against one wall with coffee pots and fixings for family and guests. Suzanne allowed that her sense of direction was better than she had thought. As she passed into the reception area, she was aware of a man and woman near the front windows and automatic doors, quietly -- but very publicly -- arguing with each other. The man was dressed oddly in an orangey-brown tunic and pants. The lady, with her long blond hair and fringed jacket just looked a bit out of time and place. She looked familiar to Suzanne, but Suzanne couldn't place from where she might have known the woman.

"No, you must leave her alone. You've upset her and I won't have it!" the man said in a hushed but still vehement voice.

"I'll see her as long as she wants to see me. You are neither her nor my boss. Remember that!" the woman countered.

Murder at St. Katherine's

Suzanne was curious and anxious to hear more, but between the couple's turning away from her, more towards the picture windows, the automatic door to the outside opening and closing with other people coming and going, and the phone at the reception desk ringing, she was only able to hear snatches of the conversation.

"That was then, this is now, let it go!" The woman said.

"Never!" the man countered.

Then there was an unintelligible exchange.

"Stay away!" the woman said. Suzanne wondered if the woman might not be in some danger from this man, but as Suzanne watched, the man kept his hands to himself and did stand a bit away from the woman, giving her room, but making him have to speak a bit louder than he probably wanted to, explaining why Suzanne was able to hear what they said. The woman then quickly put a coat on, rummaged in her handbag for her car keys and left through the front door, leaving the man standing by himself watching after her.

The show apparently was over for now so Suzanne turned back to the coffee station. The coffee pot was full of fresh coffee, a good sign. She poured a coffee into one paper cup and added two sugars and cream. Then she poured hot water from the other pot over a teabag and one sugar in another cup for herself.

Bill arrived at the rehab center at that point to visit with Ann. He planned to update her on the robbery case, even though the robbers had made a clean getaway and he personally did not feel the robbers would risk capture by striking again. Chalk it up to a bad evening, and a case unsuccessfully concluded. They didn't get all the criminals all the time. He had gathered up what magazines he had at his small apartment, brought the arrangement of three small poinsettias his great-aunts had sent him, one from each of them, and a tin of freshly baked cookies that he had taken the time to bake mid-day. He'd left his kitchen in a bit of a mess, but he would deal with it later. First things first. Upon arriving, Bill saw the coffee station. Perfect. After three years working together, he knew how Ann liked her coffee, so he'd take her a cup to have with his cookies. As he approached the station, an attractive woman turned away from it, concentrating on the coffee cup in each hand, nearly colliding with him.

"Oh, sorry!" she said, her espresso eyes twinkling, her short black hair falling into her eyes.

"No, sorry, it was all me," Bill said quickly, "Sorry." And then watched as she smiled broadly at him, turned and went back down a hallway out of sight.

Bill felt a familiar buzz along the edges of his brain, a fizz in his ears, a warming in his chest. Was it her smiling eyes, was it her amused voice, was it how her coloring and hair matched so well to the tailored and expensive black and red outfit that she wore?

Bill had come unprepared to jot all this down. No notebook and pen in his hands! He had all but given up recently with his writing. There never seemed to be enough time or energy to do a good job at it. He felt that in the last few years the toughness of the job had almost beaten the words out of him and chased his muse away. Right now, he felt a familiar pressure mounting behind his eyes. He knew he had to get all this down on paper. Tonight, at home alone, he'd write once again, the words flowing and tumbling over each other like a spring brook.

He walked into Ann's room and found Ann dressed and sitting in her chair alongside the bed. Much to his surprise, he also saw the delightful dark-haired woman from the coffee station. Being an investigator, Bill did not believe in coincidences as such, but he did believe in the serendipity of life. Perhaps this was one of those moments.

Ann could see the familiar signs of something brewing behind Bill's cool facial features. She had studied Bill for three years now and recognized the signs. Yes, Bill was intrigued, was bemused, was heading down that path to becoming besotted with her good friend, Suzanne.

Now she had two coffees, and so far, five poinsettias. She told Bill to put his on the windowsill as well.

"It's nice today. Cold but nice," Bill volunteered.

"Yes, but the radio in the car indicated there is a storm coming in time for Christmas," Suzanne said, thinking to herself how pleasant this man looked and acted, and was that a faint scent of lime she noticed?

Ann would have chuckled if it hadn't already been such a long day, and if the therapy session hadn't left her weak, tired, and in more pain than she wanted to admit. Weather and storm conversation? Could these two not find something more significant to say to each other? Ann supposed it was a starting point, but come on, move it along a little bit!

She had never thought to introduce Bill to Suzanne. There were almost ten years between them in age, but maybe that would not make a difference. Bill was an old soul to begin with. Suzanne still young enough for whatever developed.

"Bill Dancer, this is Suzanne Beck, my good friend, my old college roommate. Suzanne, this is my associate, Detective Bill Dancer, about whom you have heard me speak these last few years. Bill, Suzanne was just telling me about an altercation in the lobby. Did you notice anything?"

Bill still had his eyes on Suzanne, as he answered, "No, everything seemed quiet enough." Ann let it go at that for now. Her detective juices had been resting for few days now and still did not seem quite up to speed. If Bill said it was nothing, it probably was nothing.

Bill offered Ann the magazines which Suzanne then shifted to the pile of paperback books she had brought on the rolling tray. Then Bill offered his tin of molasses sugar cookies to them both, pleased he had something to share, and that he had taken the time to whip them up before coming.

"You baked?" Ann asked in surprise.

"Yes, ma'am, my favorite childhood cookie. I just hope I did them justice. The women in my family can really cook, so I hope they are okay. They taught me a great deal growing up, but I don't get a lot of chances now to do much baking. I was the only boy born for five generations on my mom's side, so I did get schooled in many things about which young men are not usually instructed. I learned many things tagging along with my two sisters and girl cousins."

He had tried one of the cookies before leaving his apartment, and had decided they were good enough to bring along, but would the Ann and Suzanne like them? He hoped so.

"Molasses sugar cookies," Bill explained. "My mom's recipe."

"Oh my! One of my favorite things – molasses!" Ann proclaimed.

Chapter 5

December 22

At three o'clock the next afternoon, Robin left her mother's room at the Rehab Center and followed Suzanne to her car, a late model red Nissan. Robin smiled. Suzanne liked red. She wore a lot of red, especially as an accent color. Robin knew that it was because of her black hair. Red looked good on her. Robin always leaned towards blue. Being blond and blue-eyed, she knew that blue complimented her own coloring. Robin's allowance for clothes wasn't huge, so she planned carefully to be able to mix and match many outfits and always looked put together as best she could. She studied fashion magazines and online sites for ideas. Robin liked to think of herself as a smart and creative shopper. Today Robin wore a pair of slim jeans with a navy mock-turtleneck sweater, small gold stud earrings and her boots, not the clunky snow type boots but low-cut boots made to wear with jeans. Many other the other girls at school seemed to have unlimited clothes allowances. Robin did not let that worry her.

Suzanne had always been around as far as Robin remembered. But now that they had moved to Buckelsmere, Suzanne seemed around quite a bit more because she lived so close. They rode in silence. There was no need for small talk. They both were very comfortable with each other, and silence was acceptable. Neither would worry why they weren't talking. Robin figured Suzanne had things on her mind, too.

Robin fingered the pile of music in her lap. Wonderful Christmas music. She wondered if it were all the more wonderful because they only sang it within a month's timespan each year. Then it was shelved and ignored for the next eleven months. Robin never passed up an opportunity to join in when singing was involved. The Christmas Eve services meant having extra practices, but Robin didn't care, she thrived on it. They had chosen to attend St. Katherine's when they moved up to Buckelsmere, and Robin had joined the youth choir which was giving her great enjoyment. The choir director made each rehearsal a joy, not a chore at all. She kept the young people interested and committed. She actually had taken Robin aside, and encouraged her to consider taking private voice lessons, letting Robin know that she thought Robin had talent and great potential. Robin wanted to take the lessons, but knew she would have to approach the subject carefully with her mom and John, her stepdad. She'd be asking for more money for her interests and hobbies. Robin knew that, at some point, the funds would not be there for everything that she wanted. She might have to do more babysitting or something to help pay for them. She'd ask after the holidays, when all this with her mom settled down. She also maybe had an in with a voice teacher, as her friend, Caela Marlowe, had an aunt that gave lessons. That might help the decision go her way.

Caela had a wonderful voice. Caela played the cello. Caela was the envy of everyone. With her cute figure and fun attitude, be more like Caela was Robin's desire, even though, in her heart, she knew she should just be herself, even if that person was too freckled, too tall, not so talented, and not so pert.

Robin reflected back on her thirteenth birthday, just last week, but it seemed an eternity ago. So much had happened. So much had changed, was still changing. A week ago, her mom was up and walking like normal. A week ago, her birthday and a few gifts was the most important thing. A week ago.

Robin looked out the car window, but saw nothing of the lakeshore and the houses going by. She saw visions of her mother, in the hospital after surgery, appearing so small in the bed, so pale. Robin also saw visions of Detective Bill, her mom's associate, rumpled, his face drawn, his voice unsure. Rumpled, it was the only word that she could think of to describe how she felt Detective Dancer looked. Robin was hurting, but she hurt in those moments as well for her mom, for John, for Detective Dancer. She had been so very glad to see that today her mom was more herself. Her mom had even cracked some jokes with Suzanne that afternoon before the two of them left for the choir rehearsal. Robin counted out how many more days until her mom might come home. Nine days until New Year's. She had a hunch her mom would be home before then, and that her mom would make sure that happened. Until such time, Robin and her stepdad, John, would just continue with this new daily schedule of morning school and chores and then late afternoons and supper with her mom. School would recess at noon on the 23rd until after the holidays. During the Christmas school break, she had a book to read, a report to write, and she needed to catch up on her Spanish grammar, Spanish not being her strong subject. But she'd do it after Christmas Day, Robin had promised herself. Start the 26th of December and get it done as quickly as possible. Then if her mom did make it home before New Year's, Robin would be in a better position to help. When they did get her mom home, on a walker and pretty immobile for six weeks she'd been told, it would fall on her and her step-dad to make sure her mom had what she needed, was entertained and followed the doctor's guidelines.

Robin thought about her new school. Mom and John told her a year or so ago about their plans to move from Philadelphia to Bucks County; specifically, Buckelsmere where John had found Mereswood – quieter, fresher air and cleaner water, a much better school for her, a new home for the three of them. They had promised her that she would be allowed to have friends over and give the occasional party which thrilled Robin. There never had been room for that at their city condo. The move would be in advance of her mom's eventual retirement from the Philadelphia Police Force. Robin had faced starting high school at a new school anyway, so the switch to Buckelsmere High School was no different than it would have been in the city. She might have known a few other entering Freshmen at her city high school, but the city high school would have been a consolidation of many smaller K-8 schools, so most of the other students would have been strangers. It had been what, four months already? She'd made a few new friends, joined a couple after school clubs, mostly music related, and even been to her first Boy-Girl party!

Robin smiled at that memory. She didn't know why anyone fussed over these things. It had ended up no different than any other school or church function. Boys standing on one side of the room, girls standing on the other. But she had felt very grown up that day – a new outfit, even new shoes. She'd put on a tiny bit of eye make-up and a hint of pink lip gloss that Caela had brought over to her. She wondered if her mother had noticed as there was not a word of complaint from her about it.

Of course, it could have been her mom's eyesight. Maybe her mom had not been able to notice the slight change in Robin's face. Robin had kept the makeup application light. Robin knew about the eye problems, she'd overheard enough to know her mom eyes would never improve, only worsen. Robin supposed that ought to make her feel badly, but her mother's upbeat daily attitude more or less hid that fact. Life was uncertain, as Robin had been told many times, so Robin would just roll with the currents, like her mom and John seemed to do, aspiring to feel that same inner peace Robin sensed in her mom and John.

"Turn here," Robin instructed Suzanne as they neared St. Katherine's Church. "The driveway isn't really obvious from this direction."

"Thanks," Suzanne said, navigating the Nissan through the stone wall into a brush edged lane, although she was aware the passageway was there. Twenty feet along, it opened up into a parking lot, already filling up.

Suzanne had driven the three miles from the Rehab Center north into the center of the Buckelsmere, then right on a side street to St. Katherine's, in silence, taking Robin's lead. No need to press the youngster into conversation if silence was what she wanted. Robin must be dealing with a lot right now. Suzanne wondered how much Ann and John had shared with her. She had known Ann since they were college roommates: so many confidences, hopes and dreams as well as their fears and nightmares had been shared for a very long time.

Suzanne had been completely surprised when Ann had arrived home from Scotland with baby Robin – she hadn't seen that coming. No one had. It seemed a sudden and life-altering decision on Ann's part. But it had turned out okay. Ann, John and Robin were proving to be a very secure and solid family unit. Suzanne felt a pang of jealousy over this, but knew she was being silly. Yes, she was widowed, her dear Frank killed in Iraq. Both her parents and Frank's parents had passed away as well. Suzanne had been left financially well off, but alone. Unbeknownst to her, Frank had arranged a surprisingly large life insurance policy early in their marriage. She still missed Frank, even fifteen years after his passing. Her memory of him was still strong, but it was now just a memory. The initial stabbing pain of his loss had tempered over the years. There were no tears now. Just a loneliness.

Suzanne parked and opened her car door, Robin giving her a quizzical look.

"I'll just stay until your rehearsal is finished. Maybe I can help with the programs or something for tomorrow," Suzanne explained in answer to Robin's unspoken question.

Robin gathered up her music, pulled her coat tighter around her against the biting frigid wind and then headed to the door of St. Katherine's Church. Inside the narthex, and out of the cold, Suzanne unbuttoned her coat and looked around for something obvious to focus on or to do. St.

Katherine's was an old stone church, very traditional in appearance with a separate narthex, the main sanctuary through the swinging doors. It was an old-time sanctuary with vaulted ceiling, center aisle and two side aisles, oak pews, and stained glass. Through the little window in the door to the sanctuary, Suzanne could see the ladies of the Altar Guild being busy with the greenery and linens for the altar in preparation for tomorrow night. She would offer to help for an hour or so today and tomorrow while she waited for Robin.

There was a couple dozen young people all milling about, talking with each other while they waited for the rehearsal to start. The door to the robing room, off to the left, was still locked. Suzanne supposed that the choir director hadn't arrived yet with the key. Robin had explained that the choir would start in the robing room, then they would practice their processional and, once in position at the front of the church, they would practice the music for tomorrow night.

There was a loud clatter behind Suzanne, through the doors dividing the sanctuary from where they stood in the narthex. She took a quick glimpse through the crowd and saw a janitor, mopping up the floor where the kids had entered. He moved along, swinging the mop from side to side, head down, silent. Oddly familiar. Suzanne wondered if she knew him. It was his orangey-brown clothes that especially made her think this. Suzanne believed it was the same man she had seen at the Rehab Center earlier that day – the man arguing with the woman in the lobby. She studied him for a few more seconds, until he moved out of sight and down a hallway. Something dark, evil, and unchecked was present here. Suzanne felt it as strongly as if it had slapped her cheek. But the slap had not been real and the feeling began to pass. She shuddered. Perhaps it was just her being silly and over reacting to the melancholy of another Christmas alone.

"Mark the Monk."

Robin's voice startled Suzanne, and she jumped. Suzanne hadn't noticed Robin standing so close.

"What?"

"That's Mark the Monk. I heard some of the other kids talking about him. He's the new janitor here. Some kind of Monk, can't remember exactly what kind. Maybe the kind that makes the fruitcakes. They say he killed a man," Robin said, seemingly unaffectedly. "I wish we'd get started. I hate when these things are all disorganized. Where is Chloe, I wonder?"

"Really, Robin! Killed a man? What kind of talk is that? And he's not the fruitcake type – that's Catholic, this man is obviously not a Catholic based on his robes," Suzanne said.

"It's what the other kids said. I have no idea. I just steer clear of him. He gives me the creeps," Robin shuddered. She knew more about murder and mayhem at thirteen than most adults. After all, her mom was a police detective, and Suzanne was sure tales were shared at home.

Chapter 6

December 22

Mark continued on his way, mopping and cleaning up. He wanted to look busy and necessary, to have a reason to be in this part of the church today. He had decided he would confront Chloe again. He couldn't wait any longer. His goddess Vajrayogini! His Tibetan female Buddha, whose transcendent passion was to lead him to a place free of selfishness and illusion, changing his overly strong earthy passions into enlightened virtues. When he had first met her, so young and pure and golden, he had known she was the One. The One that could do this for him as nothing else on earth had been able to. Then that night, the night Ron died, as she stood before him and the others, her unbound hair flowing around her, her hands on the driguk, their ceremonial knife, stained with blood, Mark felt her full and true spiritual power surging through him. And now he had found her. He once again would be able to meditate, now that he was in her presence; and he would recite the goddess' mantra that he had committed to memory so long ago. Mark would say it over and over as he had so often in the past fifteen years and he would listen deep within himself for her reply.

Murder at St. Katherine's

Lady of Trauma, Lady that absorbs pain
Ascetic and bhairavi and sannyasini and mistress
Pull me from the disaster that I have made of my life
Save me from the evil machinations of others.
Saviour, Lady, Mother Goddess, Bodhisattva,
Love me as I love you
I am desperate and bound
Free me by your grace.

I will give freedom, but not without realization
Those who have been bound, bind others
Those who have suffered, cause suffering
I let them know how they have been affected
But also how they have affected others.
I do not wear bones because of death
I wear them because they represent what is beneath the surface
The blood that I drink is evil karma of those that I save
And the karma is then halted and does not pass to others.
I appear wrathful as I take on anger, hatred, fury, and the desire to destroy
Which are destroyed within me.
I am a dancer upon the pain of all mankind
I destroy the dark and corrupt.
My compassionate side is hidden
But for those whom I love
Who have taken on my dark grace
I open a path of shining light
With pain and sorrow left behind.

He *must* speak to her; he *must* reclaim her! She must open that path of shining light for him! Mark continued to mop and started to work his way to the left side of the narthex where he knew Chloe would head to get into the robing room with her young choir already assembling there. Mark kept his eyes open; he didn't want to miss her in the throng.

Suddenly she was there, every bit as beautiful as when he'd first met her fifteen years ago, when they were so much younger, when so much had not yet happened. Chloe, her still girlish figure, her long blonde hair free and loose down her back just like she had always worn it. Mark felt the aura around her, her status of goddess still emanating from her. She had not lost that at least during the three years they had been apart. It thrilled him. He desired her all the more for it. His desire rose, surging through him.

Mark propped the mop up in the corner of the hallway and waited for her to come closer. He straightened his robe, the same robes he had always worn, the same as she would remember him wearing. He must secure himself back in her transcendent presence. He should never have let her leave Texas to escape him.

Having arrived a few minutes later than she had planned, Chloe was hurrying. She unbuttoned her coat, then swung it off as she walked. When she saw Mark standing there, a bit in the shadow, a bit in the light, she slowed, not sure if it was him or the shadow of a ghost dredged up from her encounter with him earlier. She thought she had left him and everything connected to him behind her when she fled in the aftermath of Ron's death. Chloe went to the door of the robing room and unlocked it for the young people waiting there.

"Mark," she said as she turned towards him.

"Chloe, at last you are here, and we are together again," Mark said softly, his eyes wide and glossy. It frightened her even more than his fervency this afternoon at the Rehab Center when she had gone to see his mother.

"No, we are not 'together again', Mark. We were finished years ago. I told you that this afternoon. Why are you continuing down this road?"

"I searched for you for years. When you left Texas without a word, I knew it was my punishment. I searched for you and I eventually found you – here, in this village, in this church. You are the same Chloe, the same incarnation of – "

"No, I am not! Stop all this talk. That was a long time ago, I have given all that up. I am not your goddess and I am not your wife. I want nothing more to do with you, with the Meditation Center, with Buddhism, with those terrible years! You must leave here, leave me alone, and never come near me again! I couldn't believe it when I heard you were in the area, that you brought your mom all this way. This afternoon I told her I was sorry about everything because I always liked your mom. She was always so nice to me."

"Chloe! Impossible! I am yours; I will be your spiritual mentor as always, and you will guide me through the passions that unfortunately still control me, you will guide me towards my enlightened self."

Chloe could see that Mark was not really listening, his mind was somewhere else, imaging things as he wished them, not as they actually were. His pressure, his insistence that she return to him had no effect on her. "Nonsense. So much bull. I am no goddess now, and I wasn't then either. Not then, not now. I was young, impressionable and you filled me with ideas and conceits until I started believing it myself, for way too many years. No, Mark, I will not involve myself any further with you, nor with the Meditation Center, nor with the Buddhist way. How many times must I say it? It would be better for you to give up this job and leave me alone, better for you and certainly better for me. Frankly, I think that you are delusional!" Chloe said, attempting to move past him, through the doorway and into the robing room.

Mark grabbed her by the shoulders. His smile was gone. His eyes had gone black – no light of love lingered there now. He held her tightly.

"Let. Me. Go. You're hurting me," Chloe said.

"You will never leave me again!" Mark said forcefully, as he thrust her away in release.

He had found her. She was here. She *would* be his again. He had found her. She was here. She *would* be his again. Mark repeated the words over and over to himself. A new mantra – one to use and repeat from now until Chloe was his again, back in his life where she belonged. Back where he could consider her his goddess.

Chloe struggled out of his grasp and leapt towards the robing room door. There in the brighter light and in the company of twenty odd teens, she felt she'd be safe from Mark, at least for now.

How had he found her, she wondered? How had she slipped up? It had been three years since she fled from Mark, from the Meditation Center that Mark ran, and from the memory of that terrible night that Ron had died. She shuddered and tried to stay in the present, in the now. That time had passed and was no more, she told herself. And after the Real County Coroner's office had come down with the verdict it was just a tragic accident, she didn't waste a second, and was on the run from Mark and his influence.

But Chloe couldn't help herself. She allowed herself to think about it for a minute or two. She opened her mind to the memory of it. She once again remembered the curved ceremonial blade that was in her hands, glistening with blood. Ron's blood. Her husband of two years, Ron had proved a terrible match. Yes, he was a brainy Dartmouth grad. Yes, he had lots of money made from his career in technology. But as a husband, he was a failure. He was cold and violent. And that night of the blood-letting cleansing ceremony – Chloe still to this day was not entirely sure how it had all happened. Ron had beat her, tortured her both mentally and physically at times during their short marriage, but she'd stopped him that night. That night and forever more. That's what *she* believed happened. Chloe believed she had struck out and killed Ron. She remembered only snatches of it, but had been quickly coached by Mark to stick to a simple story, not deviate from it, not embellish it with any other facts or thoughts. She was to say it was an accident, a terrible accident. Keep everything else about Ron, their relationship, Mark and the Meditation Center to herself. Give the law enforcement people nothing with which to work.

Mark had been right there, as had been many other retreatants. Later they all assured her and the Sheriff that they saw it as accidental. That was what had probably saved them all. Twenty witnesses swearing it had been a freak and terrible accident. If Mark had told them all to say it, they would have, she knew that. But Chloe was never 100% sure – the missing memory, the missing minutes. Had the others been instructed by Mark to say this to protect her? She wondered. Mark was so adamant that she should tell his version of the story. She was quite unsure what version of the story *was* true at this point. Over the last three years, therapists that she had consulted insisted that with time it would all come back to her. But so far it had not, and she was glad it had not. She did not want to be able to recall the look on Ron's face – the surprise, the panic, the pain. She did not want to recall what she might have been feeling at the start of the ceremony, and then what she decided to do while holding that knife, faced at that moment with Ron and his continued abuse.

One thing she did know was that she wanted nothing to do with Mark and the secret marriage they once had before their plot to get Ron to invest in Mark's Meditation Center. Chloe wanted nothing to do with any of that now – Buddhism, the phony lives of those people embracing it, the unseemly relationships that Mark had with countless other young Goddesses as he called them. Done! Done! Done! She had decided after those days of constant police interviews and then Ron's cremation and ash scattering, that she was done with all of it. Convinced she'd just wasted thirteen years, two marriages and with blood literally on her hands, she was done!

Sneaking away wasn't her style, but Chloe knew at the time she had no other choice. She had to get away. Mark was possessive and delusional enough to somehow make sure she never left. So, one dark night, the moon having set hours before, Chloe left with just her backpack, silently starting off down the dirt road towards Dawson, Texas, the nearest town.

She knew she'd given herself enough time to get into town on foot before her absence was discovered and understood for what it was – *escape*. There was plenty of time to get away before Mark discovered she had left and took action to drag her back. At first light, Chloe was sitting in a diner with coffee, waiting for her chance to get out of town. When she saw a feed delivery truck driver come in for three donuts and a large take-out coffee, she knew this was her best chance to get herself out of the desert. It had been easy hitching that ride, for it didn't matter in which direction it took her, as long as it was away from Mark. From Dawson, she went south on US 83 and then east on US 90 with the truck driver to San Antonio. Then she caught the first flight back to the East Coast and life as she remembered it: seasons, green countryside, enough water for showering and flushing a real toilet. She hadn't realized how she had missed real plumbing and plenty of water during those thirteen years living in a yurt in the desert. No more rituals, no enlightenment, no sordid sex for gain or to calm Ron's temper or to satisfy Mark's exhausting need for her. No more. She was never going back to that.

After a string of low end, nothing jobs in New York City and Philadelphia, Chloe felt safe enough to secure this choral leader/organist job in Buckelsmere. During the last three years on her own, she had renewed her piano and organ skills. Giving piano lessons to children for cash under the table, she lived meagerly to begin with. She knew there were always church organist jobs open wherever she would want to go. Since taking the position at St. Katherine's in Buckelsmere, Chloe had found a lot of beauty and peace in the countryside here. She'd even let herself get a cat – something alive to love. Cats don't lie. Cats don't compromise your soul. The little black kitty was really all she thought she'd need. Until she met Josh Sauder here at St. Katherine's Church a few months ago. He was Chief of Police of all things. Ironic. Truth was, she had nothing against law and order. Nothing at all. She'd admitted to herself that on occasion she had come close to if not actually overstepping the line of justice, but that was all years ago, in her past life. This was who she was now – Chloe Bower, church organist, choir master, girlfriend of the Chief of Police, regular law-abiding citizen, cat owner for God's sake!

But now that Mark had found her, Chloe questioned whether she could carry on here. Maybe she should run again. How far could she go and how long would it be before Mark tracked her down again? It took three years this last time, how long would it take him the next time? Probably the internet would again give her away. No, she had to convince Mark to go and leave her alone. When she learned Mark was here in Buckelsmere, working here at St. Katherine's, she had confided in Josh one night at dinner about her past in Texas at the Meditation Center and had asked his advice, to see what Josh thought she could do to get rid of Mark. Chloe had hoped confession to Josh would be good for their relationship as well. She liked Josh. She liked the kind, decent, hardworking man she felt Josh to be. She liked him and she could not say that about either Mark nor Ron. She was mesmerized at first by Mark, submitting to him and his decrees and plans, even to the point of divorcing him so that three months later she could marry Ron for his money at Mark's insistence. Money that she knew Mark needed to keep the Meditation Center operating. But she could not say she ever liked Mark, and she certainly had never liked Ron. His fits of rage and everyday displays of meanness had left her bruised and crying far too often to like the man.

She gathered her thoughts together and then got on with the task at hand. She ran the choir through the processional, then each choral piece several times. First together, then just the girls, then just the boys, then altogether again. She'd be playing the organ during the service, so she needed the choir ready to sing with a minimum of actual direction. When she was satisfied, and with a quick look at her watch, she dismissed them with the admonition to be on time for tomorrow afternoon's rehearsal.

Chapter 7

December 22

That afternoon, after Suzanne and Robin had left for the first of the extra choir rehearsals, and when the strangely garbed man had left the old woman in the room next door, Ann could once again hear soft sobbing. It was impossible for her not to hear. And after a few minutes, it became impossible to ignore.

When Ann had her occupational therapy session earlier, the therapists suggested she stay dressed after her shower and remain sitting in the chair by the window instead of getting back into bed. They had a plan for her rehab so she'd be ready to go home next week. Ann agreed with them, the sooner the better, and sooner wasn't soon enough! The pain seemed to be lessening, which was a very good thing. It encouraged Ann to be a bit more active.

So, when the woman's sobbing got far enough under her skin, Ann pushed aside the rolling tray with the magazines, books and cookie tins on it, reached for her walker and a couple of the Christmas oranges she had wrapped earlier, and decided that a short shuffle out to the hall and into the next room couldn't hurt.

Ann was to put no weight onto the side with the broken hip, so she shuffled along using the walker and her arms to bear the weight from her right side as she went step by step out of her room. No one stopped her, no one hollered down the hallway admonishing her to get back to her room. Life was already improving, Ann decided. Maybe she would take her Christmas Eve and Christmas Day meals in the common room out near reception. Get herself out of her confining, depressing room. That might be good, she decided, and thumped her way forward.

She tried to be as graceful as possible as she approached the door to the room next door. Ann wanted to get very good at handling the walker to show the staff she was able to go home as soon as possible. The old lady was alone, her face turned away, but she was obviously still upset and not in control of her emotions.

Ann tapped on the open door. "May I come in?" she asked quietly, so as not to startle the woman.

The old woman nodded, wiped her eyes and tried smiling. Ann was encouraged, shuffled in and got close to the old lady in the bed. The woman gestured to the one chair. Ann debated standing for a short talk, or sitting for a longer visit. Sit, she decided, her curiosity getting the better of her.

"My name is Ann, and I brought you a couple Christmas oranges," she said, producing the tissue wrapped oranges from her sweater pocket.

"Thank you so much. Please set them over there on that table. I don't get visitors, so I am afraid I am unprepared to reciprocate."

"No need. I do the oranges every year. Reminds me of my childhood. We always had an orange or an apple and a handful of mixed nuts in our Christmas stockings. Now, many years later, I realize it was an homage to my parents' childhoods, and the Christmases of my grandparents as well. At the turn of the last century when my grandparents were tots, and during the depression when my parents were children, Christmas was not what it was for us growing up in the post war bounty. An orange was an exotic and welcome treat for them. There were no oranges in the stores, they were transported especially for the Christmas season from Florida. I have tried to learn that lesson, that bounty doesn't necessarily make magic. Sometimes it's the simple, pure pleasures that are the best ones. I make sure we all still have an orange at Christmas. I remember my granddad with every orange I give away. I try to picture the joy in his face as a child, being handed such a treasure.

"And of course, many would say the orange harkens back to St. Nicholas as well. The legend of St. Nick. He was born in what we know as Turkey. He was wealthy, but decided to devote his life to helping others, rising up through the church and eventually becoming a Bishop. Legend has it that St. Nicholas learned of a poor man that could not find suitors for his three daughters. He didn't have money for their dowries, so no eligible men were interested in marrying the three poor sisters. St. Nicholas traveled to that man's house and secretly tossed three sacks of gold coins down the chimney, one each for the daughters' dowries. The gold happened to land in the stockings of the girls that were hanging next to the fire, drying. These oranges that I share today are a symbol of the gold coins that St. Nicholas gave away that Christmas. And of course, this led to our modern-day Santa Claus stories of bringing presents down the chimney."

"That's such a nice story. I have never heard it before. Broken leg?" she asked.

"No. Hip," Ann said economically, "You?"

"Heart, so they say. I don't know. My son says I must be here, not home alone. I'd rather be home," the old lady's eyes started to fill up again.

"Your son, he's the gentleman I see occasionally?"

"Yes, Mark Ayers. You've probably noticed he appears, well, different. He's a Buddhist of some sort. Gosh, I don't know why he left the church and went off on this Buddhist thing. But it's been years and years now," the old woman reminisced. "Do you have children?"

"One, a daughter."

"Then you know. You have plans, a vision of how it will be – school, college, marriage, grandkids, holidays, vacations at the shore . . ."

"Yes," Ann said economically, knowing the less she said, the more she could draw out of this woman.

"He took this turn, I guess it was right after college, after working for a few years. Mark was very successful, but gave it all up. He went on some enlightenment weekend, and then, well he got sucked in and he's now some kind of swami, some kind of monk. I remind him occasionally, he's not good at it. He doesn't keep all their rules nor the vows he took."

"No?" Ann asked quietly, moving the conversation forward.

"No," she said, then quietly so no one else could overheard added, "He was secretly married and this girl was so besotted with him she agreed to his secrecy terms. Married, but no real marriage. The lived allegedly celibate," a knowing look passed between them, the woman cocking her head ever so slightly in a I-Know You-Know kind of way, "in a yurt of all things in the Texas desert. He had decided to start and run his own Meditation and Enlightenment Meditation Center. Catered to the rich and successful, used his own success as a draw. Once in, he'd allow them to support the Center, as he liked to say. Support, my eye. I know he must have socked it all away somewhere, all those funds. How expensive can yurts be, after all?"

"This girl he married; she is here with him?" Ann asked.

"Chloe. Her name, Chloe. Sort of. We were all in Texas. Mark had me living close to him, as close as Mark could find me an apartment, which was a bit of a distance, but at least I saw him occasionally. I guess he tried to be a good son and pay attention to me, but it was very lonely in Texas all those years. I am a New Yorker, so fifteen years in the desert, the lonely desert, the hot dry desert, was hard to take. When he said he was moving East and I was to come, I was so happy. Ecstatic, at first anyways.

"But when we arrived, he quickly put me here, in this place," she said, looking around at the bare, institutional room, "saying I wasn't well enough to be at home alone." Tears started again. Ann reached over and touched her hand. The old lady grasped Ann's for a few moments while she struggled to get her emotions back under control. Ann could see the anger, the disappointment, the loneliness. She had to choke back sympathetic tears herself.

"Perhaps this is only temporary, until Mark knows you are fit and well enough to come home with him," Ann suggested.

"No, I fear the worst. I will be here until I die. I will be here for what's left of me. I cannot bear to think on that."

"What does your doctor say? Can you perhaps come out to the common area out by reception, meet people and enjoy some of the activities they offer the residents?"

"Oh, Mark wouldn't like that. I did the first day or two until he came in and saw I was out there. He became very angry and made it very clear I was to say away from anyone. I don't know what upsets him so greatly about my having friends. There's a lot of folks just like me here and none of them should worry Mark."

"What about this girl, this Chloe? Can she not perhaps intervene for you, put a word in Mark's ear about you and your needs and wishes."

"Chloe," the woman said, "I liked Chloe, but she was so young, so taken in by Mark's strong and domineering ways. I think she liked it at the beginning, but after years of living with him, secretly married, they up and divorced! She said in the legal proceedings that the divorce was because he was unfaithful to her. Yes, there were lots of other women more than eager to submit to him, lots of other goddesses as he called them, I knew about that, but I tried so hard to ignore it. But truthfully, I think that it was a divorce of opportunity. The Center started out as a Mediation Center but towards the end, I think it had turned into more of a cult. Anyway, Chloe divorced Mark, and within two months of getting the final decree she was remarried to some wealthy tech guy from Long Island who had expressed an interest in the meditation, enlightenment and peace that the Center advertised. So, Chloe and this man – Ron – married, moved to the Center, and there she was, once again within Mark's grasp.

I liked Chloe. She was always so sweet and warm towards me the few times we did see each other in Texas. But that didn't please Mark. Mark didn't like his people interacting with the outside very much. Not even Chloe with me, her mother-in-law. Control – that is what it was about. And all his insecurities. Then there was that terrible accident –"

"Go on," Ann encouraged.

"That man, Ron, that Chloe was married to, he ended up dead after some kind of exercise or ceremony or something. I never did really get a clear picture of what happened. But he was dead. The coroner came back with an 'accidental death' verdict. There was a ceremonial knife or sword or something, and he accidently was fatally struck by it in the chest, and died before they could get proper medical help from the nearest town. He bled out."

"Who . . ." Ann dared ask.

"Chloe. Chloe claims she had the knife. She said it slipped and accidently hit this man, her husband. Hit him square in the chest."

"Unfortunate, but if it was indeed an accident," Ann started to say but was cut off.

"I don't believe it for a moment. That's the horror of it. I don't believe any of it. You see, there had been talk by what neighbors there were of unusual ceremonies. Bloodletting ceremonies, odd communal get togethers. Oh my, I cannot even say the words!"

"Bloodletting? That doesn't sound very Buddhist," Ann commented.

"No, Mark strayed way too far from the teachings he was to follow, and I think some of the things that were practiced at the Center were of his own invention to satisfy whatever he was needing or dealing with inside himself. Some of it was unnatural and appalling!" Mrs. Ayers confided.

Ann was beginning to get the picture. This poor woman had suspected all this, and borne it alone, all these years. Ann squeezed her hand again, hoping to draw the woman out of that dark past and back to the light and green starkness of this room. The woman choked over the next few words, but had apparently decided to relieve herself of all her secrets to Ann, all at once, since she had a sympathetic audience and the opportunity.

"Now I have discovered we are not here in Pennsylvania for the peace and quiet, for the wonderful history and interesting people – no, we are here because Chloe is here. After the accident, after the investigation and the verdict of accidental death, Chloe up and disappeared. At first, God help me, I suspected, I was afraid she had met an untimely death herself, somewhere alone in the desert mountains near the center. No one would ever find her body. No one would ever know. I feared that these last three years. Mark was beside himself that he had lost her, that she was gone. It seemed his emotions were true, but too over the top. But so much had happened, I feared . . . that he . . ."

"Yes," Ann agreed, "I can see you must have had many suspicions, and no answers. No one to answer them even if you had asked the questions."

"All this time since then, I guess Mark had been looking for her. I don't know how he found her, but he did. Here in Buckelsmere. Next thing I know, Mark canceled the lease on my apartment, handed what was left of the Meditation Center over to his 1st lieutenant, or whatever you call the second Buddhist in charge, and we set off across country to get here. I thought our lives were going to turn around, change, go back to normal. Mark seemed so happy to be leaving Texas and come East. But I didn't know it was because he had located that poor girl. Poor Chloe."

"Do you think perhaps she contacted him?"

"No, I don't. Mark's euphoria ended recently, after we had been here a few weeks. Mark took a very small apartment, a bed-sit, and plunked me in here. I think it was to get rid of me from his everyday life. And now -- I think perhaps his intended reuniting with Chloe is not going as he planned. He has taken a janitorial job at a church, St. Katherine's -- "

"I know it," Ann interjected.

"He doesn't need much money, but he has to have some income since he left the Meditation Center behind. We are here to be near his goddess, as he calls her and now, I fear again. I fear for my son because he is so unhappy. I fear for myself stuck in this place, and I have to admit it, I fear most of all for Chloe. After three years, she must have moved on, gotten her own life back again, looking towards her own future. She's young still. Sadly, I have to say I am sure it does not and will not ever include Mark or me. She came today. She must have learned he was here chasing after her in Buckelsmere, and I was in this facility. She basically just came in to see if I was okay, and to tell me that she had no intentions of picking back up with Mark. She would let him know as gently as she could.

Ann was worried all this talk was agitating the woman past her capacities. She knew this was all family, personal stuff, but Ann felt an affinity towards this lonely, worried woman.

"I tell you what. I have to be here myself until at least New Year's. I will practice on my walker and come every day after your son leaves for work, I assume. We can visit without him becoming overly concerned and angry about it. How would that be? And maybe things will look a bit brighter. What do you say? It would help me out, too."

"You are so kind. Too kind. But yes, please do. Mark works late afternoon into the early evening at St. Katherine's. And with the extra holiday services this week, he has to be there for all those as well. I would welcome your company."

"Good. I will plan on it. Maybe if Mark is not here at dinner times, you'd consider letting the staff take you out to the common area, sit with others and if nothing else you'd have a different four walls to look at."

"Okay, I'll think about that."

Ann took her leave, slowly shuffling back to her own room. But the buzzing Ann heard in her brain, the police nerves that this woman had aroused would not easily settle down. There was trouble here.

Bill. She would call Bill.

Bill had managed to check in at the station that morning, but there was nothing more for him to do, he'd been told. Just stand down while Internal

Affairs did their thing. Guns had been drawn and fired, but no one injured by them. Routine stuff. So, it was just a matter of time before he was cleared to go back to police duty. Now at home, he cleaned up the kitchen mess from his baking the day before. Bill liked his kitchen ship shape.

Bill was starting to feel better about things after his visit yesterday to Detective Essex in the Rehab Center. She looked more like the Detective Essex that he knew. And of course, he'd met Suzanne about whom he'd spent a good deal of time wondering. He should keep his mind on with getting through the investigation, seeing how Detective Essex was faring, and dealing with Christmas, but he was hoping he would see Suzanne again, maybe this afternoon. But now, with the kitchen cleaned up and no police work to finish, he'd sit and try to get more writing done. More words on paper. This was his focus for the time being.

His three great aunts, his maternal grandfather's sisters, had hoped he'd be home for Christmas, his mom had told him on the phone yesterday. Bill would be very sorry to miss seeing them. He'd make a point of seeing them over New Year's weekend. He'd take them some Champagne. He made a quick note to do so on his desk calendar. He'd pick up a couple bottles before he left the city on the 30th of December, heading west to the family's farmstead. Bill knew they wanted him to join them at a writer's retreat in the fall. But that seemed so far away, he couldn't bring himself to think about it. Writing. Yes, he had to get back to his writing. His three aunts wrote collectively under the name Tria Petras, the Three Stones, much like other famous authors that were actually two or more people, like sisters Lynne and Valerie Constantine writing under the name of Liv Constantine, husband and wife writing team Nicci Gerrard and Sean French using Nicci French; Ellery Queen was the pen name of cousins Daniel Nathan and Emanuel Lepofsky. And that's what Bill's aunts were – Helen, Dot and Jan Stone, living and writing as one as Tria Petras. They were popular and successful writers, as they hoped and wished Bill would be. He couldn't fault the old dears on their affection and good intentions, but it would be up to him in the end.

Which led him to once again face the Big Question. What did he really want to do – police work or write? He knew he probably could not make a living being a detective fiction author. But this city detective job was more overwhelming than he had originally planned. It seemed to be days sometimes between his opportunities to sit and write, making it very hard to keep any sense of rhythm and moving forward.

And now, with Detective Essex being laid up for the foreseeable future, Bill was not looking forward to working with the heads of other detective units. He knew he'd be farmed out to one of them. He had gotten used to Detective Essex and her ways. He felt he could anticipate what she'd need or suggest, and because of that he felt he was usually on top of things.

At the Rehab Center the next time he saw her, would he dare talk to her about this? If he knew her plans, he might feel better about making his own plans. But in the end, he knew he would have to decide for himself, regardless of what Detective Essex might decide for herself. Bill began to suspect she might decide to call it a day after this, but he could be wrong. Maybe she'd make plans to retire, if she didn't already have those plans in place. He wouldn't blame her. Last June he'd gone to their housewarming party and felt it was such the right decision for Detective Essex, her husband John and daughter Robin. A big stone farmhouse to absorb their attention and energy, better schools for Robin. A lot of peace and quiet. In total contrast to the grit and bleakness of fighting crime on the streets of Philadelphia. Bill did not know yet what he would do if she left him alone on the force. He'd have to man up and face it if it happened, he figured. Three days from now was Christmas Day. He was alone, in the city, with no plans. So, he'd write, and be thankful for these few days to himself.

He had taken the cookies that he had baked yesterday and had been pleased how they had been received. So today he'd sit and give some effort to his writing. Sitting down as his desk, Bill always wrote at a desk, he smiled as he opened his black leather portfolio to look at the meager stack of pages that he had written the last couple of days. But he was writing again, and that was the important thing, not the word count. Maybe it was the adrenalin that surged during the pursuit of the jewelry robbers, or perhaps the shock of having his boss fall hurt during the chase, or perhaps it was meeting Detective Essex's friend, Suzanne. He would write her into his current detective story. Hmmm . . . the possibilities.

But more likely it was that Bill had received a letter the day before from the publisher of major detective fiction magazine that had recently published one of Bill's stories. They were contacting him to ask for additional stories. Best Christmas gift of all time! Where he so recently had felt lost and wandering without creative direction, he now felt focused again. Now, he needed the time and energy to get on with polishing and submitting some of this detective stories to this magazine and then finishing the novel that was sitting on his desk.

Bill's cell phone rang, pulling him back out of his reverie. He gave it a quick glance, hoping it was nothing and was surprised to see Detective Essex's ID put up. He quickly answered it.

"Yes, ma'am?" he said by way of hello.

"Bill, I need you to do something for me. Some research. I can't do it myself in here," Ann said.

"Sure, anything," Bill said, pulling a clean sheet of paper out of a drawer, "tell me."

Ann hung up the phone after talking with Bill, more at ease now, knowing that Bill would be up to see her in the morning with the information she requested. Bill was very good at research even if his chasing robbers left something to be desired, she chuckled to herself.

The day was drawing to a close, soon there would be dinner on a tray. The thought of the unappetizing meal was depressing. Thus, Ann's spirits were raised when Suzanne and Robin returned from the choir rehearsal with several piping hot, fragrant pizzas from her new favorite pizza parlor. The smell of sausage and onion, pepperoni and peppers, goat cheese and prosciutto – heaven on earth! Ann hadn't realized how hungry she was. She must be starting to feel more herself, that and having been switched from the opioid pain killers to over-the-counter pain killers today helped her appetite return, she was sure.

And, just then, John arrived with the mail, Christmas cards, and another poinsettia, this one from her sister, Jane, in Baltimore. Ooooh, fun! Ann realized. She'd leave the card that came with it in plain sight so Bill would see it in the morning, to tease him just a tiny bit. Ann knew that Jane had spurned Bill's small advances that he had made after that weekend adventure three years ago. No other woman seemed to have entered into Bill's life since then. Ann did want to see Bill happy in that respect, but knew a cop's life did not lend itself to a happy and stable home life without an awfully lot of effort, patience and love on both partner's parts. Although the windowsill was getting a bit crowded with the various colors, sizes and shapes of the poinsettias, Ann pointed towards it, directing John to place it over there.

After Ann had looked at the cards, John started taping them around the edge of the white board. Then he sat and started a crossword puzzle. He did the New York Times' puzzles, and he did them in ink.

"How was rehearsal?" Ann asked Robin.

"Oh, fine. You know," Robin answered, distracted by the pizzas and a couple of young orderlies going down the hall past Ann's doorway.

Suzanne moved closer to Ann so she could speak quietly. She had decided on the short drive back from St. Katherine's that she should fill Ann in.

"There is talk among the young people in the choir, that the janitor killed a man. I am not sure what all that is about, but it can't be good. If it's true, can it be safe to have him around? If it's not true, it seems a bit cruel for the kids to be believing it. And," Suzanne paused, looking around to see who was within earshot, "I think it's the same man I saw her earlier today, in the lobby, arguing with Chloe, the church organist."

"Ah, yes. Mark the Monk," Ann said.

"What? You know?" Suzanne asked in surprise. But she knew she shouldn't have been surprised. Ann's police "nose" was always at work.

Chapter 8

December 23

The skies were graying up when Bill arrived late the next morning at the Rehab Center. Snow was coming, he thought. It would be a difficult drive home tonight if it did snow, as he had found that the Philadelphia region and suburbs did not do a very good job at snow removal. The theory was to just give it time, it would melt on its own.

He pulled into a parking spot, gathered up his portfolio of notes and printouts, and climbed out of the car. Bill almost never wore a hat against the cold as it did bad things to his hair, which Bill preferred to always be looking neat and dignified. He did button up his coat to the top button. He shivered as he felt the slow, penetrating, damp coldness. The colder it got, the damper it seemed, until the snow would start. Bill tried to gauge how long until it did start. Bill hoped it wouldn't snow at all, but snow was forecast as a definite for Christmas Eve.

After Detective Essex's phone call to him yesterday he'd spent the rest of the day and this morning tracking down and talking to local Sheriff of Real County, Todd Russell, in Dawson, Texas. Bill had written his report, printed out a few substantiating documents, photos and maps and had them ready for Detective Essex. Why Detective Essex had asked him to do this he had no idea. He'd find out soon enough. When Detective Essex shared things, she did. When she held things back, it was always for a reason. Today, Bill was guessing it was so that she did not prejudice the information Bill would discover and relay to her, so that Bill was open to all and everything he was told and could ferret out of the Texas law enforcement system.

Entering through the automatic doors, the warmth hit him first, then the Christmas music playing off to the side of the lobby, and then the chatter between staff, residents and visitors. It seemed almost reasonable if you could ignore the old and crippled who were hunkered down in their wheelchairs as he passed, and the closed doors of patients who could not or would not join in any festivities this Christmas season.

He stopped at the reception desk, picked up his visitor pass and then proceeded to Detective Essex's room. How many more days would she be in here, he wondered? The doctor had said two weeks. She had told him about a week. He was privately wagering closer to four or five days if she had anything to say about it.

The door to her room was swung open. Detective Essex was sitting in the one chair in the room, her walker nearby. Alert, she greeted him with a smile, which didn't quite reach to her eyes, still taunt with the pain she must be feeling, but trying hard to ignore. He realized every little thing must be a terrible effort for her.

"Bill, come in. Drop your stuff, see if you can locate a second chair. They keep taking the extra chairs away. You'd think they'd realize by now that I need extra chairs in here. I'm assuming and I'm hopeful that you have a great deal to share with me, and that it may take us a while to get through it."

"Yes, ma'am. You are correct on that. An unusual and, if I might add, an extremely disturbing case." When Bill returned with the extra hard chair, and had placed it close enough to Ann to pass papers back and forth, he sat and reached for his portfolio.

"Bill, before we start. There is something I think we need to discuss," Ann started. Bill froze, the hairs on the back of his neck rising. No, not yet, not now, he wanted to say. Let's just continue on, please, he wanted to beg her.

"Bill, you don't have to call me Detective Essex. Just call me Ann," she said. Casually, as if it were a cast-off remark. As casual as flicking a crumb off her lap. It took Bill an extra couple of seconds to digest that her request was as simple as that. No hidden meanings, no portents of disaster ahead. Just her request for a more informal relationship. At least for now, he told himself. Once back at the police station, he knew he'd revert to his old ways. But okay, for now, Ann it would be.

"Okay, Ann," Bill said economically. "By the way, no sign of the jewelry robbers."

"I figured. Long gone, for sure," Ann said.

"I think so, too."

Ann nodded once, then continued. "You know how I like to do this. You take it from here and tell me everything that you have learned, no detail will be too small, include everything, even what you suspected was being said to you but was not put into words. Tricky, since you did the interviews over the phone, but there's no time and no resources to go all the way to Texas to do personal interviews like we should have. And," she added, "this is not an official investigation. Yet. I hope it never will be, but there is something, something my mind cannot let go of, and it's nagging me."

Bill nodded and started his narration of yesterday's and this morning's phone calls and online research.

"Mark Ayers became involved with Buddhism after his Dartmouth years at some point. My Texas sources were unclear on exactly when. First, he practiced Buddhism and taught Enlightenment in New York City, then decided upon opening a spiritual Meditation Center in the desert in Texas. I guess because of the cheap land and the lack of worldly distractions. He rented quite a few acres of desert outside Dawson, Texas, nothing for miles around but cactus and rattlesnakes. Pretty barren and actually a hard life to maintain as there are so few resources at hand, so it took money. So, Mark pandered his particular brand of Buddhism to the wealthy, specifically to burnt out New York City executive types. They would come to Texas, start to feel unencumbered, and Mark would help them out further by lightening their pockets. It took money to build the yurts, to provide the water and sanitation systems, and make these people feel like they wanted to stay. What few neighbors there were, occasionally complained to the local Sheriff. They said there were weird rituals going on, blood sacrifices and odd behavior in general. Not that they had any quarrel with Buddhism per se but, in their minds, the whole thing there in the desert just didn't seem right.

"The sheriff said that there had been an accident involving the group, he called it a cult, a few years back. A man had been fatally wounded in a ceremonial knife ritual. He thinks it was incorrectly ruled accidental, but could find no evidence or convince anyone who had been there that night to admit it had been murder. He just had a feeling that information was being withheld, and the real story wasn't being told. A man was dead from a knife wound to the chest. There were twenty witnesses that swore at the time that it was only a terrible accident and nothing else. When the judgement came down as accidental death, the sheriff said he felt disgusted, but knew he couldn't really do anything about it. Undermanned as so many rural law enforcement units are, he had to just move on to the next case.

"The Meditation Center has fallen on hard times since then. Mark Ayers' investors and then his devotees started to leave when provisions started to run low. After all, one does need to eat to be able to meditate. Without money coming in, Mark found it hard to provide even the basics.

"Sheriff Russell said that he thinks no one remains in the desert at the Meditation Center. The wife of the dead man, one Chloe Bower, disappeared immediately after the inquest. Packed everything she could carry, closed the bank account, took all the assets her husband had not already given over to Mark, and for all intents and purposes, vanished. Sheriff Russell did express his feeling that perhaps she would have been better off if she left a long time before that. She'd spent ten years as the main consort to Mark to the dismay of the Buddhist community at large. Even the Dali Llama contacted Mark to tell him to knock it off and get back to the pure life. They had taken a vow of celibacy. Supposedly, there were a lot of other young women also eager for validation by the head guru."

Bill produced a photo of a much younger Mark and his golden goddess girl, Chloe. He, vibrant, tanned, strong. She, golden-haired, young, dressed in white flowing garments. Ann studied the photo silently, absorbing the faces, the implied emotion between them, the power of a photograph from so many years ago. She looked back up at Bill, signaling him to continue.

"Sheriff Russell said that the ceremonial knife here in this photo," which he passed over to Ann, "was some kind of Samurai looking thing that was used by Mark and the group in blood-letting ceremonies, but somehow one night it got out of control and whatever they did went too far and a man, Ronald Bowers, ended up bleeding to death before help could arrive." Bill consulted his sheet of notes. "It took twenty-two minutes between the initial call to emergency services and the arrival of a paramedic. It was a long way out there on very bad roads.

"I spoke with a Ms. White who had been there that night," Bill said and looked up at Ann with laughter in his eyes. "She still lives nearby and runs the Karma Dog Grooming Service. She says that Ron was known to beat Chloe. Mark had taken him to task several times about it. It seems Ron had issues with the fact that Chloe and Mark had been together for ten years, and that Ron did not know about it until well after his marriage to Chloe and his move to the Meditation Center. Must have been a bit of shock. You marry a girl, you convert to Buddhism, you give over a fortune to a man who is supposed to be your spiritual leader only to find out this guy had been sleeping with your wife for ten years, before you were suckered into this situation.

"Chloe had not been completely honest with this Ron from the start. He apparently had a temper that he was finding increasingly hard to control being faced daily with Mark's presence and Mark's pressure to hand over his worldly goods for the Meditation Center's use. The group of residents had all been there that night, the night of the accident. It appeared to all of them to be no different than any other night when they performed that same ritual or ceremony. But something happened, the blade slipped, or it was accidently flung or dropped, it changed position when it should not have. It happened so fast no one anticipated the problem. And, suddenly there was way too much blood. By the time they realized they needed help and found a phone that would actually pick up a signal out there, it was probably already too late. Ron was dead before the paramedics arrived. This Ms. White said she felt that Chloe deserved a better life than either of these two men gave her, and wasn't surprised to hear that the Center had probably closed down. I couldn't see her eyes or watch her body movements, but it has been so many years now and I think she was telling me the truth as she saw it, not just repeating something she'd been told at the time to tell the police."

Bill nodded at the photo, obviously a police evidence photo. It was an interesting item, with a curved blade, an ornate silver handle, overall about fifteen inches long, with a particularly pointed and sharp looking end. Ann looked from the photo back to Bill.

Bill knew what she was thinking. "Sharp. Not a toy. Not just ceremonial. And," Bill said with emphasis, "Sheriff Russell said that it has disappeared. Gone. Pouf. Not in the evidence box any longer. He had pulled the box in advance of my call when he learned I wanted to go over the case with him. He did say that perhaps the judge on the case sent it back to the Center once the verdict came down 'accidental'. If so, any one of a number of people could have it now. He has no idea at this point, but it is gone. He said he'd look into it, but it was a case from three years ago, and frankly I wouldn't think it is too important to him now."

Ann's brain was going a mile a minute, compiling thoughts, ideas, questions. But she'd wait until Bill was finished presenting his research.

"Even more interesting, Sheriff Russell says all of this was recently brought up, discussed and shared with," Bill paused to check his notes to make sure he had the name correct, "one Police Chief Josh Sauder of the Buckelsmere Police Department. Recently, like last week. Sheriff Russell was very interested what might be going on here in Pennsylvania to generate all this interest in a case that was put to rest three years ago there in Texas." Bill paused looking at Ann and let it sink in. "Someone else locally seems extremely interested in this story," he finished, closed his portfolio and sat back in his chair.

Ann took a couple of minutes to absorb the last couple of details. Then she asked Bill, "So, let's see what we have so far. A Buddhist monk, Mark, selling his enlightenment Meditation Center services to high paying executives. He has a cache of young women devotees or whatever you want to call them, one in particular that he is secretly married to, I'll tell you more later about that later," Ann explained to Bill, "This girl, Chloe, after ten years divorces Mark, marries a rich New Yorker, Ron, within months of the divorce. They end up back at the Meditation Center. Mark then starts to work on Ron to get him to hand over his money. Ron becomes increasingly violent towards Chloe. Mark pressures even harder. Then one night, when she can take it no longer – a slip, a cut or two, and Bob's your uncle. Once exonerated, she flees with the money, refusing to give in to Mark's demands and obsession over her."

"That about sums it up," Bill said.

"Not exactly," Ann said, wondering how much of what she now knew and suspected she would share with Bill. Was it not perhaps just her wild imaginings? He was right here, his mother was here, Chloe was here. Chloe who had gotten close to Robin. What sort of danger did this all put her precious Robin in? What sort of danger, Ann wanted to know?

Needed to know. And why were the Buckelsmere Police Department interested in all this?

There was a stirring of air, a sudden waft of light lily fragrance, and Suzanne was there in Ann's room with them.

Bill stood, "Hello."

"Hello," Suzanne said to him and Ann. "Am I interrupting something, anything?"

"No, no," Ann assured her. "I didn't expect you until later."

"Well, I was meeting CheChe, you know my friend Florencia, for lunch. Gosh, it's tough to eat out so close to Christmas in this small village! Everything is either closed or closing up for the holiday! Don't they know some of us need a meal, I mean, really!" Suzanne shared her frustration to Ann's amusement. "So anyway, I digress, after a quick Thai curry, CheChe had to leave to stop and pick up something she ordered at the bakery, and I decided I'd just come on over here, to see if you needed anything this afternoon. I'll be back in a couple hours to pick Robin up to get her to her rehearsal. And tomorrow for services. Rather looking forward to it, actually. It will give me a reason to get out and go to church tomorrow night. I am rather afraid that otherwise it would be just be me sitting home alone with a cup of eggnog."

Bill found it hard to believe such an attractive woman would be alone on Christmas. He cleared his throat and ventured in at the shallow end.

"No family here about?"

"No. Sadly. No," Suzanne answered.

Ann thought about the simplicity of that quiet cri de coeur. Alone. Alone on Christmas. Her best friend had been widowed early in life, early in her marriage to Frank Beck and hadn't found any one else to replace him. They only knew what the State Department had told Suzanne. Frank was in Iraq as a civilian consultant in geospatial intelligence, having his Master's Degree in that field from Penn State University. He was installing some equipment, and there had been an ambush. No matter how few details she knew, it was still the same outcome. Frank had died,

Suzanne was alone, and life would never be the same. Ann and others had rallied around her. Ann had been Suzanne's main shoulder to cry on, to confide in, and finally to show an inner courage and strength of acceptance. Suzanne eventually decided that moving on with life was necessary. She was very young, still in her twenties at the time, and had a lot of life left to live. It was hard to believe it had been fifteen years ago, time had passed so swiftly.

And here was Suzanne now, dark hair recently styled, her face happy with the upcoming holiday, in her red Christmas coat and diamond snowflake pin, speaking quietly of being alone to a man who would also be alone. Ann understood 'alone', having faced the depths of the meaning of that word on several occasions herself. Truly alone. It could be soul destroying, or it could be the source of a magical inner life force.

Ann wondered if this was what Mark was feeling. Alone, no Chloe, no Meditation Center. Alone in a place foreign to him. Was his resolve stronger, were his desires and obsessions also stronger and more destructive as a result?

"Have a cookie," Ann suggested to the two standing in front of her, eyeing each other, with nothing more that they dared say to each other.

"We were just wrapping up here," Ann explained. To Bill she added, "Let's see if we can get a hold of this Chief Sauder and see why he's asking questions about this situation." Ann was not yet ready to suggest any other action to Bill. There were still things she needed to know. Good police work did not spring out of half-cocked ideas and conclusions.

"Chief Josh Sauder? Oh, that will be easy," Suzanne answered licking the crumbs and sugar off her fingertips, a lovely red that matched her coat. "Chief Sauder will be at St. Katherine's later. He's dating that Chloe Bower, the choir director and organist."

Bill and Ann exchanged a slow, long, steely look. Nothing else needed to be said.

"What?" Suzanne asked, "What did I miss?"

"It's a little involved, and I am not sure where the whole thing is going, but there is something, something about to happen that I can't put my finger on yet," Ann explained. To Bill she added, "As I was going to tell you, yes, Chloe is here. Mark is here, and his mother is next door," and nodded towards the wall separating the two rooms.

Suzanne was not surprised that even now, broken hip and all, Ann was working, her detective juices were flowing.

Chapter 9

December 24

Christmas Eve day dawned gray and still. After another early breakfast of oatmeal and weak coffee, Ann was helped up to shower and dress, then do an hour of rehab -- of shuffling along the hallway on her walker and going up and down a mock set of stairs, practice for when she would go home. She knew they were watching to see if she'd be able to handle the staircase before they would give her the okay to go home.

Once back in her room, Ann decided to evaluate the situation. Maybe nothing would happen. Maybe she was being oversensitive because of the accident, the surgery and the medications. She knew she was still feeling shaky. But her family, her friends and Bill did not need to know that nor worry about it. She'd been down before and always fought her way back up to fly again. She wasn't known as the Phoenix for nothing!

Ann picked up the sound of soft low whimpering from next door above the hallway clatter of rolling carts, wheelchairs, the odd early visitor wondering down the hall stopping in to visit their old and infirm friend or relative. She decided she needed to talk to Mrs. Ayers one more time, and find out if there was anything additional that Mrs. Ayers could contribute. Ann got herself out of the chair by her hospital bed, grasped the walker and started for the hallway.

As she arrived in Mrs. Ayers' doorway, Ann had to feel sorry for the woman. She was alone, still in bed, sobbing into a tissue again. Maybe just Ann's presence would alleviate this poor woman's depression. Perhaps not. Ann knew she needed to stay focused as a police detective would, but sorrow is hard to ignore. Ignore it often enough and one became cold and callused, cynical and unauthentic, bad at the job.

Both tissue-wrapped oranges were still on the rolling tray, untouched.

"May I come in?"

"Yes, please," she said, wiping the last tear swiftly with the tissue.

"Your son is not coming this morning? Maybe later for the caroling program in the lobby area?" Ann asked

"No. I haven't heard from him since yesterday when he left here midday. It is so unlike him. He has been attentive in his own way. He comes every day; he makes sure I have what I need. He never has much to say, but I think that is because his life here in Buckelsmere is so small in comparison to who he was in Texas at the Meditation Center – some big Buddhist enlightenment guru. His job here is menial, I know, but it pays for his rent and his food. He does nothing else. He comes here, then goes on to work at St. Katherine's, then home to his tiny apartment for a night's sleep. I am worried why he has not come today, especially since it is Christmas Eve."

"Perhaps the church had extra work for him because of the services tonight and he is there. Maybe he thought he mentioned that he's not coming. You'll see, he'll come and tell you all about his day at the church getting ready for tonight. It will be fine. Try to keep a smile on," Ann suggested, not totally believing what she had said herself. Ann was sensing a rat, somewhere close. Something was amiss since Mark's pattern had changed.

"It's just that he's been so quiet these last several days. Even more so than normal. Withdrawn. Pensive. All that previous happiness I saw in him seems to have totally evaporated."

"Could it just be the holidays? They affect a lot of people that way. They promise happiness but only seem to accentuate loneliness and disappointment. Maybe having been away from the church for so long has left Mark unprepared for what Christmas has dredged up emotionally for him."

"Maybe. Maybe, you are right and I ought not to worry so much until after New Year's when everything is over and he will be back to a simpler daily routine. And maybe that will have been enough time for Mark to either reunite with Chloe or accept that it is over. I mean, it has been three years since she left him and all that tragedy behind. I think she has managed to move ahead to the next thing in her life," Mrs. Ayers said.

They talked for a few more minutes about the weather and how the forecast of two inches of light snow might affect Christmas Eve and Christmas Day for everyone. When Ann felt she had spent enough time talking about innocuous things to get Mrs. Ayers out of her funk, she gathered her courage she needed to hoist herself out of the chair and back onto the walker, making her goodbyes.

"Now, eat that orange, and think happy, positive thoughts for the rest of the day," Ann said in parting.

In the hallway, Ann passed a man and woman heading towards Mrs. Ayers' room. Not Mark, someone else. Not a doctor. Maybe from the church? He was with Chloe, whom Ann recognized right away from church and Robin's singing functions. Chloe had taken an interest in Robin and had spoken to Ann privately once about the possibility of Robin taking voice lessons -- age appropriate and not too strenuous for her age, but with a classical repertoire that Robin seemed to favor. Robin would be ready for that this year or next, so Ann had discussed it with John as a possible activity to give Robin one more thing here in Buckelsmere to help her feel part of the community.

But this couple being here at the home, here together but without Mark around, here to see Mrs. Ayers set off alarm bells in Ann's head. Something was up. Developments were underway. And if Suzanne was correct, was this not the Chief Sauder that they needed to talk to? Ann would not know until she got back to her room and googled him on her laptop. If it was Chief Sauder, there would be photos of him on the internet from news articles, local political events and the like.

They went into Chloe's ex-mother-in-law's room, sat and started to talk with the old woman. Ann could not hear anything specific, but imagined it to be a short explanation that this was the last time they'd see each other as Mark was not part of Chloe's future. That the man she had with her was Chloe's new boyfriend.

Josh had come for moral support. He had encouraged Chloe to come and give herself closure in her relationship with this woman. In Chloe's confession to him the other night about her past, her relationships, and the death of husband number two, she had expressed sorrow over abandoning this woman who had always been kind to her. Chloe thought she owed it to Mrs. Ayers to explain and say goodbye – as much for the old woman as for herself. Get past it and move on. Josh had seen the wisdom in that, and encouraged this trip back to the Rehab Center specifically to get it over with. Josh wanted Chloe done with Mark and his mother. Josh did not want to be sharing Chloe with any ghosts from her past. Thought of Mark always being around, harassing them enflamed Josh. Chloe's telling Mark it was over, and her goodbye to his mother now – would that be it? Would it be over then? Mark out of the picture and Chloe all his? A dream come true, plans to be made, a bright future. At Josh's age, this romantic relationship with Chloe came as an unexpected but very welcome occurrence. This woman attracted him like none other had ever done so. He was thinking about their future together, perhaps marriage and children. His chest swelled when he envisioned it. He would be able to hold onto Chloe unlike that punk fake monk, Mark. Josh could not even begin to imagine what Chloe had seen in the man. Punk fake monk. That's how Josh thought of Mark. Let her *say* goodbye, Josh was going to make sure it really *was* goodbye.

John and Robin arrived to spend the afternoon with Ann before Robin left to go to St. Katherine's with Suzanne to the early Christmas Eve service. Soon after, Suzanne popped in as well, thinking it would be easier to arrive before any snow did. At least one leg of her day's driving was done without any snow. John rose to find more chairs, but Suzanne insisted she wouldn't be there long enough to worry about it.

When Chloe and Josh were leaving, and passed Ann's room, they couldn't help looking in at the cheery group, handing a box of cookies around, and helping themselves to the tissue wrapped gifts, and settling down for ham and cheese sandwiches that John had fixed for them. He said it was to supplement the lunch that may or may not have been adequate, and to fortify them against whatever might come for dinner.

Robin saw Josh and Chloe pass by and quickly looked at Ann with a look that Ann wasn't sure how to categorize – not fear, maybe just apprehension, or confusion?

"Mom, that's Chloe from St. Katherine's. Why is she here?"

Ann weighed in her mind what her answer ought to be. "I think she knows the woman in the next room. She's the mother of Mark, the church janitor." Always best to just tell the truth, the simple truth, whenever possible.

"And that man was Chief Josh Sauder," Suzanne added. "You and Bill were looking for him yesterday. Such a shame they are gone, and that Bill isn't here – I could have made introductions," Suzanne said. Ann wondered if in this day and age does one actually make introductions? But then was quickly brought back from her ruminations.

"Mom, Chloe is seeing Chief Sauder. She's with him if you know what I mean."

"Oh, yes, Robin. I might be old, blind and gimpy, but I am familiar with the jargon," Ann teased her.

"So, I don't really understand. Yesterday, Mark had a terrible disagreement with Chloe at church, demanding she return to him. Let me see, his exact words were 'you are the same incarnation of my goddess' and after some mean words, he grabbed her, mom, he grabbed her and said, 'you will never leave me again'."

Sandwiches midway to their mouths, Ann, John and Suzanne stared at Robin for a few seconds in silence, absorbing the ramifications of what Robin had overheard the day before.

Ann wet her lips before speaking, trying to remain calm. "Did anyone else see and hear this?"

"I am sure of it. It took place outside the robing room. There were plenty of us in there already and more coming all the time, and there were parents and other church staff about."

"Robin, are you sure this what you heard Mark and Chloe saying? Really sure?"

"Yes, or I would not bring it up now. I wouldn't have bothered saying anything if I hadn't seen Chloe with Josh here today. I mean, you know, people have arguments and say stuff they regret later all the time, right? No need to make a federal case about it," Robin answered.

Suzanne added, "I didn't hear it. I must have already gone into the sanctuary to help the Altar Guild ladies with the decorating."

Ann thought hard for a minute or two. She did not know where all this was leading, but her sixth sense was saying it would lead to trouble eventually. The eternal love triangle never ended well. "John, maybe Robin ought to stay here tonight, not go – "

"Mom! Don't be ridiculous. I'm going and singing. Everyone will be there! I won't have much of a Christmas otherwise. I'm going!" Robin asserted.

Ann knew she had to let Robin go, even in spite of the less than adult-like outburst. She was only just thirteen and friends had told Ann that it would get worse before it got better with a teenage girl, so pick your battles.

John tried to quietly temper the mood. "What can happen? She'll be in church with hundreds of others, never alone, never in any danger. Suzanne will be there," Suzanne nodded exaggeratedly, "and we are five minutes down the road. Maybe Bill can go, too, if that would help you feel better about it. I don't know his preference of religion, but just about anyone can enjoy a Christmas Eve service with carols and the Nativity scriptures being read out loud."

Ann relented. "Okay, go, sing. Suzanne will be there. I'd send Bill, if he were here. I don't know why he isn't here yet. Come back here as soon as you can, though." Ann didn't want to add that she had a dark feeling about it all. Very dark. And she wondered where Bill Dancer was. Where? Ann needed him here.

Chapter 10

December 24

It was very quiet after Suzanne and Robin left for St. Katherine's. Very quiet between John and Ann. Ann took some pain medication, hoping it would help with more than the pain she was feeling in the right hip. She knew she'd overdone the physical activity today. The pain seared all the way down to her ankle. Ann asked John for some hot tea to help settle her stomach and her nerves. He left to fetch it for her, while she sat and prayed. Please God, let Robin be safe tonight.

Robin was only thirteen, at the start of her teenage years, her great journey towards being grown up. Please God, let Robin be safe tonight and come home to us. Ann wasn't exactly sure what she was fearing, what she expected to happen, but there was a feeling, a feeling she could not ignore. Not at all a Christmas Eve fireplace and mistletoe kind of feeling. It was almost an itch, a crawling of the skin without reason, this sense of foreboding, the premonition of violence. Ann had always been sensitive about things, and had often been compared to her great-grandmother who had the sight. Ann tried to stick to the real-life facts and figures. Occasionally though, her intuition was so strong she dared not ignore it. On those occasions it had proved fruitful. Ann had learned not to talk about it as it usually led to scoffing by family and friends. She especially did not mention it at work.

John was a quiet person normally. Ann knew that he understood her moods and her needs very well after these seven years together. John and Ann were easy together, not making demands of each other. They really never needed to as they were more often than not on the same wavelength. They both were analytical in their approach to things, list makers, and believed the joy of an event often lay in the preparation. They sometimes even dressed the same without knowing what the other had already chosen. Ann and John laughed together a lot; the joy of their life together too great to contain within themselves.

Ann had met John at an Amish farm stall at the Reading Terminal Market where she often bought fresh produce before returning home to her apartment and Robin in the evenings. They both reached for the same head of cauliflower at the same time, their hands touching. They laughed and decided that Ann should have the cauliflower, as John really didn't need one quite that large anyway since he was cooking it just for himself. One thing led to another and pretty soon they were cooking for more than just themselves. Ann had been very cautious before becoming involved with him. She had learned that so many people had such hidden putrid pasts, and she was not subjecting Robin, still just a child, to anyone not suitable until she really knew that person. Time did tell the story eventually, and Ann married John willingly and completely. She had not felt sorry for a moment since.

Before John returned with the tea, Bill arrived.

"Snowing," he said economically.

"I hadn't noticed. I hope it doesn't get bad too soon. Robin and Suzanne are at the church," Ann said.

Bill could hear the tension in the simple words.

"Do you want me to go? I could. Just in case they need me to drive them later on?" Bill asked.

John returned with the tea, and exchanged a quick hello with Bill. Bill was putting his coat and gloves into the closet, not being one to haplessly throw them in a pile somewhere.

"It's snowing," John said as he handed the black tea to Ann. John had seen more of Bill in the last week than he had in the three years previous, and realized he quite enjoyed the younger man's presence.

"So Bill has said. What do you think, should Bill go up to St. Katherine's? I was thinking if he'd been here when Suzanne and Robin left that I'd have asked him to go along. Am I being silly? Have I lost my grip on reason because of the surgery and everything?"

"No. I think Suzanne and the rest of the congregation can get through one Christmas Eve service without your sending the cavalry in," John joked. Bill chuckled on cue. Ann smiled, trying to feel happier, pushing the memory of the vision of the robed and hooded man far back into the recesses of her mind. She did not want to dwell on what that earlier vision might mean.

"Bill, I saw Chief Sauder this afternoon. He was actually here, at this Rehab Center with Chloe. Chloe had come to visit Mark's mother. I suppose Mark let on that his mom was here, and Chloe decided to visit and let Mrs. Ayers know not to expect any further contact. Maybe she even asked Mrs. Ayers to intervene and tell Mark to back off, that she really was done with him. Maybe Chloe figured that Mark's mom could make an impression on him, where maybe he was not listening to her. Josh must have come along for the company, to support her, whatever. More likely because he found out that Mark had gotten physical in an argument with Chloe yesterday. Yes, that's right. Robin apparently overheard it all. Josh might have been acting as bodyguard bringing her in here, not knowing if they might run into Mark. He hasn't been in to see his mom since yesterday morning," Ann looked at Bill to see his reaction, which was that he pulled back away from her an inch or two. That was Bill's normal reaction when something really significant was revealed and he didn't necessarily want to say anything. Yes, Bill understood the situation was not good. Ann nodded her head to him.

"I couldn't get Chief Sauder on the phone at the Buckelsmere Police Department's offices earlier. He was out, unavailable. I left a message, but he hasn't returned my call. Now I know why," Bill said looking at his watch. "Too late now to be able to get him, especially if he is at the church for services. Tough on a holiday to nail people down for interviews when no crime has actually been committed. We have no right, no jurisdiction here. Rather frustrating. Tomorrow, Christmas Day, will be a loss, too. I guess we wait until the day after Christmas; see what develops. We'll get to the bottom of why Chief Sauder was asking the Texas sheriff all those questions.

In the end, Bill stayed with John and Ann, in the quiet early evening. Dinner arrived on trays. He knew had he gone to his parents' house, he'd be sitting down to Roast Turkey and Duck with all the trimmings tonight, their traditional Christmas Eve fare. He would have helped make the Roast Beef dinner tomorrow for the extended family, complete with Yorkshire pudding, the choice of roasted or mashed potatoes, four vegetables, his signature horseradish sauce and his grandmother's chocolate cake. Right now, though, Bill knew he needed to be here, with Ann and John, keeping a lid on things and a watchful eye cast around. Food could not be his focus.

Bill thought about the future now. His doubts lately over staying on the city police force had fully blossomed after Ann's accident. He did not want to ever go through something like that again. Would Ann return to the City or pack it in at this point? She had quite a few years in, but maybe not enough for a full pension. John was obviously well heeled enough to support them comfortably from what Bill could tell. Bill had foreseen the eventual end of their partnership coming when John and Ann bought the farmhouse and moved, allegedly because of Robin's schooling. Yeah, right. He'd seen through that story. She was setting the wheels in motion to retire and this jewel robbery episode would prove the catalyst to bring that about.

Did he want to go on for a while longer without her, with a new supervisor? Short answer, no. Yet, he wasn't going to back to the farm either, having thought about it for days and ruled it out. Bill had fifteen years invested in police work. He wondered what that meant towards a pension. It would be nice to get another five years in. But could he do this for five more years? He wasn't earning enough yet from his writing. 'Yet.' He always said, 'Yet', trying to think positive, to make positive things happen. Thoughts churned in his mind, whirling around and around. Bill kept hoping, with each passing day, that answers would present themselves.

After a while, Bill got up and said he'd take a walk. He left the room and headed towards the lobby. There should be other people there, and music, and the Christmas tree. Maybe that is what he needed. A little Christmas.

As he walked, Jane sprang into his thoughts. Bill had seen the card from Jane that came with one of the poinsettias. It has been left out in plain view; he couldn't miss it. Ann's sister, Jane, red of hair, fair of face. And funny too. After that weekend, when Bill was moving to Philadelphia three years ago and had met Ann and her family at that country inn, he had tried to start a relationship with Jane, but she never seemed willing to reciprocate. Baltimore was close, but not close enough for the match to work out. He realized now that he maybe hadn't tried as hard as he should have, but it was too late now.

He recognized that he needed a new plan. He felt no one would hate him if he decided to explore something with Suzanne. Why not, he asked himself? Buckelsmere was close enough to Philadelphia for it to work. He put his hand out to touch the Christmas tree, saying to himself that if it was a real and not a plastic tree, it would serve as a good omen. Bill fingered the needles at the end of the branch. It was real, bringing a smile to Bill's face.

He thought of his three great aunts, no doubt sitting down to dinner with his parents right now. They had asked him to commit to joining them at a writer's conference next fall. It had seemed too far away to make plans, but by golly, he would! He'd call them in the morning, wish them a very Merry Christmas, and tell them he'd join them! Which meant that yes, he must buckle down and write more seriously and consistently. The novel he had started would get finished and perhaps with their guidance and connections, someday it might even get published. Decision made about that at least. He'd go back and work at the Philadelphia Police Department until he knew about Ann's decision to also return or retire, and press hard on finishing the novel in the meantime. Bill felt sense of relief wash over him. Decisions were made -- at least for now.

During Bill's absence, John removed all of the dinner trays to the hallway, straightened up the room, rearranged the poinsettia plants to make room for the two additional ones that had arrived on the last florist's delivery, and helped Ann into bed which relieved some of the pain of sitting in the chair. Ann decided she might never look at another poinsettia after this as it would remind her too much of the accident and Christmas in the Rehab Center. She ached and was so very tired but needed to be sure all was well before kicking everyone out for the evening. Most of all, she needed to see Robin. Maybe the earlier vision of the robed and hooded man that Ann had had meant nothing. Maybe the evening would prove her senses where just over active due to her accident.

After New Year's, when she knew she'd be feeling better and more rational, she'd decide about work, but right now it was looking like she would quit. She felt like she'd lost her nerve, which could prove deadly out there on the street to herself or to a coworker. Her hip would need a lot of recovery and physical therapy. Her eyes were noticeably worse. She could not change these things. So, buck up, Ann, move on to life in this country village, house decorating, being the mother of a teenager.

Suzanne was always trying to get her interested in genealogy, so maybe she'd give that a try.

But what about Bill? She still was worried about her decision and how it would affect her junior. Ann knew in her head that she was not responsible for Bill. He was a grown man, very capable. Her leaving the detective job well might serve to improve his policing skills. He'd have the benefit of someone else's experience and knowledge and guidance. Not always easy, but often educational. Still, Ann had grown fond of Bill and thought of him as more than just a coworker. She did not want to do anything to hurt his career. He was easy to work with and they understood each other. She originally had hoped she'd be there to groom him to take her position in their detective squad, but she realized now that was not going to happen. Besides, the Philadelphia Police Department had dozens of detectives ready to bust each other's kneecaps to be able to take her spot.

She supposed she could still mentor him from up here in Buckelsmere. They could still talk. Wouldn't quite be the same though. Maybe it was time to separate, after all. There were things that had taken a great deal of her energy to keep from Bill. Maybe separation was the answer now. The secrets she kept from him, from John even, about that weekend three years ago and the death of Dr. Worthington Porter must always be kept locked away from everyone. Forever. But Ann knew in her heart she did not want Bill to just disappear. The thought depressed Ann. He had become too much a part of her daily life, but how could she safely ensure the future, how far could she trust him, how far could she trust herself to keep the secrets of the past?

Chapter 11

December 24

Suzanne pulled her car into the same parking area as before, but swung it around so her car was pointed out of the parking lot, making her exit later in the evening easier if it did snow. When she and Robin got out, she could smell the snow in the air – it was close. Suzanne hoped it would hold off, but the sky looked so laden, so dark, she knew she should wear her boots into the church instead of the adorable little Italian Ferragamo flats she was wearing. Oh, well, shoes off, boots on, snowbrush laid across the front driver's seat for easy retrieval.

Even though this early family service was at six o'clock, Robin had to be here by five o'clock for the last-minute warmups and lining up for the processional well before the start of the actual service. Suzanne decided that it was a bit of a bonus for her. She'd be able to actually get a parking spot in the lot, and her pick of pews for the service, rather than having to park blocks away on the street, wandering in later, and sitting where there happened to be an empty seat. But she'd be alone. Again, this year. Maybe she'd look for a familiar face and sit with them tonight, as if part of their festive family group. Maybe she should have asked that Bill Dancer if he wanted to come. Suzanne's mind wandered, thinking about Bill. Tall, handsome, pleasant Bill. Different from Frank. Frank had been shorter and slighter, more reticent. Suzanne always attributed his quietness to his braininess. Frank was constantly thinking about technology and work things that she knew he'd never be able to or was allowed to explain to her, so she never minded his quietness. They had been high school sweethearts and married soon after they graduated college. But it was only a few years later that he had been killed in Iraq. So long ago.

And Bill was here right now. He was taller than Frank, and his well-defined shoulders and small waistline spoke of hours working out to maintain his physique. Suzanne felt quite a curiosity about Bill. She didn't know if she wanted to admit that to herself or not. Bill seemed so loyal to Ann. Suzanne wondered if that was a cop thing, or maybe a bit of Boss Crush. No, probably not. People didn't get crushes on Ann. At least not in this century. There had been a time, back in college, when Ann was quite pursued, and would have been quite a catch for someone, if that Professor Porter hadn't interjected himself and taken over her attentions. That had been a bad time. It had taken Ann quite a while to admit it and make the break away from Professor Porter. Suzanne knew right off the whole thing was a mistake, but Ann had to come to that decision herself. Luckily, she had. Suzanne idly wondered what ever happened to Professor Porter. She'd have to look online and see if he was still a professor at Cabot College.

The interior of St. Katherine's was so lovely this Christmas Eve. The altar filled with two evergreen trees covered in tiny white lights, seasonal holly and other greenery, poinsettias, white roses, and lots and lots of candles. Real candles, Suzanne liked that. The air was filled with the scent of pine and bayberry. The altar guild had done an exceptional job this year. She could take some pointers from them. This year, she hadn't done very much decorating at her small Victorian home in the village. She'd put the candles in the front windows, which were on timers so she didn't even have to think about them. She'd put out a few decorations, but hadn't bothered with a tree this year just for herself. Seemed pointless.

Suzanne slid into a pew with a couple of older women she knew from the church's knitting circle. They wished her a sincere Merry Christmas. As families arrived, most of them with little ones, Suzanne noticed the excitement in the faces of the younger children, cheeks pink from the cold outside or perhaps with the wonderment of Christmas and what it might bring. The noise level rose to a din probably not acceptable in normal worship circumstances, but Suzanne knew it was hard to keep that many children quiet and behaving. They called this the Baby Service for good reason. Father Clement would just talk above the noise as best he could, raising his voice louder and louder as the children got louder and more restless. There would be another service later at ten-thirty. Suzanne wondered if with the forecast of snow, they would manage to actually have people show up for it. The adult choir was scheduled to sing at that service.

Robin left Suzanne at the sanctuary door and headed straight for the robing room. She had a Christmas Orange for Chloe, and some special news about one of her Christmas presents that John had leaked to her before she had left with Suzanne. She was so happy. She glowed. John had told her that he and her mom were going to let her take voice lessons starting in January as a result of Chloe speaking with Ann personally about it. Robin had been afraid that Christmas was not going to be very festive this year, and that perhaps the presents would not be up to her expectations, but this news was better than sweaters and books and the latest electronic device. Robin realized that it did seem like Christmas now. Her mom had done the oranges to give out, the church looked so very sensational all decorated, Robin had on her best red Christmas sweater and hoped her friends had news of their own of presents and parties to share. Robin decided a candlelit Christmas Eve actually was so much better than the harsh daylight of Christmas morning with just the three of them opening their presents, and then facing a very quiet day until dinner time.

"Hey, Caela, seen Chloe?"

"Hi, Robin. Yes, she went up to the organ loft to turn the organ on and get it warmed up before she comes back to warm us up."

"Okay, thanks. I have something for her," Robin said, holding up a tissue wrapped orange to Caela's knowing smile (everyone got oranges at Christmas!) and tossing a second one to Caela, "I'll be right back." She headed back out of the robing room and towards the door in the paneled wall in the narthex that led to the stone circular staircase. Lifting the latch, Robin opened and closed the heavy wood door carefully, and quietly started up the stone steps.

She could hear a man's voice above her. Chief Josh Sauder's voice. And then Chloe's voice. Unhappy, angry voices; not loud but Robin was able to hear them as the voices echoed down the staircase. Robin stopped on the last stair, not making the last turn and stepping up into the organ loft. Robin debated whether she should wait, or quietly go back downstairs. She didn't want the embarrassment of popping in on them if they were having a spat, of letting them think she was listening in when she shouldn't be.

Josh was so confident, so sure that what he'd done would convince Chloe of his love for her and she'd declare the same feelings for him. Chloe must cease being standoffish in their relationship and be willing to eagerly move forward with him. He, Josh Sauder, Chief of Police, was in control and nothing about Chloe's past would go with them into the future. He spoke to her in a low but strong voice.

"It doesn't matter anymore, Chloe, you are free from Mark. He's gone forever."

"What do you mean, gone forever? He's probably downstairs, right this minute," Chloe asked.

"Yes, he's downstairs, all right," Josh smiled wryly. "He will never bother you again. You can stay here in Buckelsmere and live as you please. I will be here, too. Together we can –"

"Josh, you're rushing things, jumping the gun a bit. No one has said anything about our future together yet. We've only dated for a couple of months. There's no commitment between us yet. We've not had any discussion about it, for God's sake. We have dinner and take in a movie occasionally when you are free," Chloe said, trying to end the conversation about the future. She wasn't even sure if she was sticking around now that Mark had found her, but didn't want to discuss that with Josh just yet.

"It is forever, can't you feel it? Say you feel it, too. After our talk the other night, when you told me about your experiences in Texas, about Mark, about Ron and about – well, about how he died – I knew I could fix this. That then everything would be okay for us to be together, forever."

"What?" Chloe asked, prickles of horror rising up her spine.

"I am the Chief of Police. Chloe, I can fix it. I have the knife from Texas. I took it from Mark yesterday. I came over here to talk with him and make him see reason. He had the knife with him, under his robe. I took it from him. I have it now!" Josh explained, his eyes narrowing and his focus narrowing has he drew the knife out from under his coat. Chloe shrunk back from him, "No one will ever have it again to be able to accuse you."

"Josh, that was just a stupid accident. I know what it looked like to the Sheriff in Texas, to Mark even, especially since I hightailed it out of there pretty quickly, but seriously, Josh, it *was* an accident. I can't believe you came here to interfere, to talk to Mark behind my back."

"Keep asserting that. That's what you need to do. Mark can no longer infer anything else; he cannot coerce you any longer to be his again. Damn him for even thinking he could!"

"What have you done?" Chloe asked in a whisper, each word separated, punctuated by the fear of hearing Josh's answer. "What?!?"

"I am afraid you will soon learn that he had a slight accident yesterday. Took a fall down the basement stairs. Careless of him. They'll find him eventually, but probably not tonight, not tonight because that would ruin Christmas," Josh answered, sure that Chloe would be pleased. Josh, full of his accomplishment and his feelings for Chloe, moved to take her in his arms. Instead, as he approached her, she pushed him off, hands on his chest, pushed hard a couple of times.

"No! I will never be part of this. I fled all those years ago, and I will not go back into being controlled by that time, that man, that knife, and certainly not you! I'm turning you in, I can't be part of this," Chloe said and started past him towards the staircase back downstairs. But not quickly enough.

Josh's anger and instincts took over. Chloe would not reject him! He could not let her do this, he had to stop her. One swift slicing motion. Just one, and Chloe was on the floor, along with a growing amount of pooling blood.

Josh thought he heard a soft thud on the staircase. In the heartbreaking realization of what he had just done to his love, Josh was not sure what he had heard, if anything. A thud? But something or someone had been there. Josh stepped over the dead Chloe to the doorway. He heard the latch lift at the bottom door and then the door close again and the latch dropped into place. Then he saw the brightly wrapped Christmas orange laying on the first step, where it had been dropped. Exactly the same as he had seen that afternoon in the Rehab Center in the room next to Mark's mother.

Damn that child! That certainly complicated things, Josh realized. She must have overheard every word, his confession of murdering Mark and maybe even his killing of Chloe. Stop, Josh. Think. Josh's mind whirled with the choices of what action would be best. It would be a child's word against the Chief of Police's. Probably not much of a battle, but it would be better just to eliminate her. So, first action would be to get out of here and snatch the girl. Then what? Dilemma there, what to do to solve that, another accident? No, too coincidental. A missing child, unhappy at home, that had possibility. Lots of teens went missing every year. He'd arrange something.

Yes, leave, Robin decided. Just as she turned, grasped the iron railing to start the twisting descent, she heard a scuffle and knew the argument had gotten physical. Frightened, Robin withdrew as quietly as she could and fled quickly down the staircase, but the orange, festive in tissue and bright ribbons, fell out of her hand and dropped onto the step. Robin was not stopping to retrieve it, and down the staircase she went.

Robin reached the robing room and grabbed her choir robe, tried to get to the far back end of the room, as far away from the staircase and organ loft as she could. She was breathing hard, her chest hurting with the effort; strokes of light flashed across her eyes. What was this, she wondered? What had she heard? Not really sure, but so sure whatever it had been, it was terrible, very terrible.

"Yo, Robin, you okay? You look a little green, or maybe it's white. Not sure," Caela asked, "And you are standing in the wrong section, this is the altos. Remember? You should be over there," Caela said, pointing towards the opposite wall.

"Caela, I feel sick. I want to go home."

"Oh, okay. I'll get Chloe and –"

"No, Chloe won't be coming, I don't think. I don't know. Caela, please, I need, I need to get out of here. I want Suzanne. Now. I can't breathe."

Caela, her auburn curls bouncing around her leprechaun face, decided Robin must really need help, so she left the robing room, figuring she still had time before the processional to find Suzanne. Caela knew Suzanne not only from seeing her around the church, but from having hung around at the Essex's home with Robin since last June. Suzanne had been around a lot, too, being Mrs. Essex's friend. Walking into the sanctuary, and up the left side aisle, Caela saw the back of Suzanne's head. She was sitting with the other knitter old ladies. Caela saw that the church had filled up, and would be full for the service that should start soon. She tapped Suzanne on the shoulder and asked her to come out with her, that Robin needed her.

There were priests and altar servers in the narthex awaiting the organ to start and then the procession. But nothing was happening. A few more minutes passed. An usher towards the front of the church was looking up into the organ loft. He then hurried away towards the back of the church and to the door that led up the staircase to the organ loft.
Then there was a scream.
When you think of someone screaming, you think of it being a woman. But this was the usher. The scream came long and loud from behind and above everyone's head, from the organ loft. An awful, loud, man's scream.
Father Clement ran up the aisle and then looked up and back where he saw the congregation looking. Then he hurried to the same doorway and staircase, reappearing in the organ loft as had the usher.
"Someone, call the police!" he yelled down.

In the end, there were no Christmas Eve services that year at St. Katherine's. There was panic. Families leaving in a hurry, children crying in fear over the rushing and screaming. The police arrived with sirens blaring, much like in the movies. Suzanne searched for Robin and finally found her with many of the other young people huddled together in the robbing room, clinging to each other, confused and scared.
The word going around was that it was Chloe Bower -- her throat cut. The usher had been taken away by the police and a medical person, presumable to be calmed down so he could answer preliminary questions. But Suzanne doubted he was going to be much use to the police. He just

happened to be first on the scene. Could have been any one of a number of people who went up that staircase to see what was keeping Chloe from starting the organ for the service. All Suzanne could think about was what Robin had said yesterday, and what Ann had filled her in on about Mark and Chloe. Suzanne just wanted to gather up Robin and get out of that place.

By the time the police had taken their names, addresses and a quick statement (no one had seen anything, had heard anything, knew anything of interest) and let them go, it was well past supper time, but Suzanne had no thoughts for food. And to top it off, it had started to snow. Robin and Suzanne lingered at the front door, looking out over the snow-covered walkway and parking lot. Chief Sauder came up behind them.

"Anything I can do?" he asked.

Robin moved to the far side of Suzanne, away from Josh.

"I don't drive well in the snow. I know it's only three miles, but – "

"Let me then. I'll take this young lady back to her parents in my four-wheel-drive, you stay here until they at least plow the parking lot. I think it's only a couple of inches so they will have it pushed off to the side soon."

"That would be so kind of you, but don't you have to stay here to deal with – all this?" Suzanne asked, a little surprised that the Chief of Police was not at this moment deep into to the murder investigation, for it had to be murder as Chloe hadn't cut her own throat. And especially since he and Chloe had been an item. She wondered how could he bear to not be there and find out what had happened? It was odd, but Suzanne did not realize exactly how odd at that moment. Suzanne was grateful for his offer so she did not have to get behind the wheel of her car just then. She knew Ann would want Robin back with her as soon as it was possible.

"It will only take me a few minutes," he answered, smiling like the fox he thought himself to be. Suzanne wasn't sure, what would Ann do in this case? After all, it was Robin – Ann's daughter – not her own daughter she was deciding about.

"Okay," Suzanne agreed, but when she turned to speak to Robin, Robin was gone.

"Don't worry, I'll find her and get her to her parents."

"I'll call them and let them know," Suzanne said.

Josh followed in the direction he thought Robin would have gone. When he did catch up to her, Robin was just about to exit through a side entrance with another young singer and her family.

"Robin, you're to come with me," Josh said.

"No. I am going with Caela. Caela's dad will drop me off at the Rehab Center. They drive right by it going home."

"Now we don't want to inconvenience them on Christmas Eve, in the snow and all, so – "

"No, absolutely not! I am going with Caela," Robin answered, much louder and more defiantly than she'd ever spoken to anyone. Could he do something to her for it? After all, he was Chief of Police. But she knew him to be a killer. She knew and she had to get out of here, just get back to her mom. Her mom would know what to do, what to say.

Mr. Marlowe said, in an effort to diffuse the tension and high emotions, "No problem, Chief, we are fine with taking Robin and dropping her off," and luckily for Robin, who just wanted to kiss Caela's dad for saying that, Mr. Marlowe then led the group out into the snowy evening and towards their car which was conveniently parked on the street right there at the side of the St. Katherine's Church.

Foiled in his abduction plans, Josh's brain was ticking over, trying to find a solution. He decided he'd get his SUV, and beat Robin back to the Rehab Center. Get her in the parking lot before she entered the building. Official Police Business, he would tell her before anyone saw her or him. He moved swiftly towards his own vehicle. He only needed to be on the road or at least arrive at the rehab center a minute or two before the Marlowe's to be able to be in position. He'd take her, stow her in the trunk, and arrive back to St. Katherine's to get that situation under his control with no one the wiser. Then he'd deal with Robin later. Everyone would wonder what had happened to her after the Marlowe's dropped her off. Only he would know.

Suzanne tapped Ann's cell phone number on her phone. Ann answered right away.

"Ann, listen, there's a situation up her. I'm sending Robin back to you via Chief Josh Sauder."

"Josh?!?"

"Yes, that's right. Because of the snow he offered to drive her and -- brace yourself -- they found Chloe murdered!" Suzanne started to explain, but Ann cut her off.

"Suzanne, it's Josh – he's the killer!"

"Oh! No! I can't believe it! What? Are you sure? Oh, my God! Robin!" Suzanne exclaimed, turning back to the church in panic.

"I'll send Bill. He will find them. Suzanne, please! Come here now!" Ann pleaded.

"I will. I will! The snow won't stop me!"

Ann's brain and heart hurt even worse than the hip. Her Robin was in terrible, terrible danger. Ann had seen this madman that very afternoon. She had not at that time figured it out, but now saw it all clearly. Ann set the phone down, looked at the two startled men sitting with her and said, "It's Josh, and he's murdered Chloe. Now he's got Robin," she explained, tears sliding down her face.

Chapter 12

December 24

Bill rose from his chair, already in motion based on the phone exchange he was overhearing and even more so based on the look on Ann's face.

"I'm going. I'll find her, don't worry," he said, grabbing his coat out of the closet and heading towards the lobby with great, determined strides. He would not let harm come to Ann's daughter. He could not!

John rose simultaneously and went to Ann, putting his arms around her, holding her, rocking her. He knew that this news, this threat would break her as nothing else in the whole world possibly could.

"John, John," Ann sobbed, "It's all too much. This cannot be happening. Please, John, do something, I can't. I am stuck here when Robin needs me the most. More than ever before in her life --"

"Don't worry, Bill is on his way there. He'll find them. He will get her back. Ann, he's a good cop, and he won't let you down. It's up to him now; we will have to trust him."

"I should have seen it sooner, seen how this was playing out, but all my attention was on Mark because he was so odd. I'm losing it, John, I can't do this anymore. I saw a monk, hooded and dark – I should have known it meant his death!"

"You don't have to do anything anymore. You don't. Don't think about any vision or dream you had, it's not real. When Robin is back with us, safe and happy, and Christmas morning dawns fair, you'll see. It will be okay," John said softly to her, rocking and holding her, wishing he believed his own words. He rang the bell for the nurse. He'd better inform them. "We'll go away when you're able. We'll take a cruise, or go to the Bahamas, or go to the cottage if that would sooth you."

"The cottage, yes, I'd like that. I need that. Maybe in August. I should be able to hike again by August. But John," Ann said, her voice rising in panic again, "Right now, we need to save Robin, and I have no idea how or where to start!"

At that second and in a whirlwind of coat, snow covered boots, flying blonde hair and flashing sapphire blue eyes, Robin appeared and flew into Ann's arms.

"Mom, oh mom!" Robin started crying, and hugging Ann.

"Robin! Oh, my love, let me see you, how did you get here? We thought –" but Ann couldn't finish, the joy of having Robin here so suddenly in her arms. Ann found herself choking back tears and sobs herself.

"Bill – Bill was just leaving the Rehab Center. He told me when I got out of Caela's car to run. Run as fast as I could!"

"Caela? John asked

"Yes. I wouldn't go with that Chief Sauder. Mom, he murdered that janitor, Mark, I heard him say so! And I think –" but Robin couldn't say it. Ann held her tightly.

"Say no more about it now. We think we know what happened. Bill was on his way to get you when we heard that the Chief was supposed to have you. Thank God, you listened to your instincts and didn't go with him. Why? Why do you think the Chief felt he ought to take you?"

"I think he knew I had overheard him tell Chloe he pushed Mark down the stairs into the church basement yesterday. I dropped the Christmas orange that I had taken up to the organ loft for Chloe. I figured that he saw it and then knew I had overheard them, that I had heard *everything*. I ran. Oh mom, I was so scared. There we so many people there and I was still so scared."

"Being scared can happen anywhere, at any time, not just in dark, lonely places."

"He had a knife," Robin managed to add.

Ann looked at John.

"Did you see anything?"

"No, I was on the staircase, just outside. But I could hear, I heard it all. He told Chloe he had a knife that he had taken from Mark."

Ann, now more in control of herself, said to John, "When the nurse comes by, I think we might need a doctor, perhaps for something to take the edge off – the pain for me, the over-excitedness for Robin, and eventually for Mrs. Ayers for the shock of what she will learn about her son. And get on to the Buckelsmere Police, just in case Bill hasn't managed. They ought to know what has happened down here at this end. I think the Chief will head here. I think he has gotten himself in so deep now, that he will figure he has nothing to lose if he finishes the job."

"You mean, me?" Robin asked.

Ann hesitated, as always summoning courage and wisdom about how to deal with Robin. "Yes, you, and others. But you are safe here. No one, I mean no one, will get to you or me or poor Mrs. Ayers next door. That poor woman, when she hears . . ."

Ann figured Robin might have gotten here just before or even just after the Chief. If Chief Sauder had seen Bill intercept her, he'd have stayed back out of sight until Bill had gone. Ann was afraid, but pretty certain that Chief Sauder was already in the building. This could turn into an ugly hostage situation with all these confined invalid patients, friends, family, and staff here tonight. A mad man with a knife and his service revolver could be very deadly.

John stepped out into the hallway when the nurse arrived to let her know that Ann needed a stronger pain killer, and that if there was a doctor on the premises, he should come at one to look at Robin who had witnessed terribly, shocking things. And that she and the front desk ought to expect the police imminently to lock down the place as they suspected trouble, perhaps violence. John could tell in her eyes that she thought *he* was the madman, but to her credit she went to do what she was asked.

Upon his return to Ann and Robin, John asked Ann how long did she think it had been since Suzanne's phone call? How long had it been since Chief Sauder had gone to take Robin and then started out in his car to get her at the Rehab Center? Ann called up the records on her cell phone, "I can tell you exactly. Twenty-five minutes. He could be anywhere, I am afraid."

"I think you and Robin ought to move to another room. Maybe down a different wing."

"Too late. He might catch us in the hallway, and as you know I've not wearing my running shoes, and he will be armed," Ann tried to joke, "We'll have to stay here. John, if you stand near the doorway, you'd see him coming and you could quickly shut and lock the door. I think that's really our only defense."

"Yes, I am sure you're right. What about Mrs. Ayers next door?"

"Tell a nurse, get her out of the way, even if it's only into the room next to her. It will stall him at least"

John buzzed for a nurse again, who came at once. John asked her to get an orderly and move Mrs. Ayers. They waited for a bit longer with nothing unusual happening. Then Ann sensed something, heard a change in the ambient noise. It got quieter, fewer voices, the music was turned off.

"Now, John. Now. Something is happening," Ann said in a hushed voice only a fraction of a second before John noticed the change himself.

Bill and Suzanne came hurrying down the hallway towards John, who stepped back away from the door. Suzanne's face was stretched tightly with concern, fear and most of all sincere regret. John waved in them into the room, closed the door and flipped the lock.

"Bill, oh my God, Bill and Suzanne! I am so glad to see you both," Ann started, "But tell me, what's happened? It is not over yet, is it? I can tell by the look on your face."

"No, ma'am," Bill started. "Chief Sauder's SUV is out front, we confirmed that. When I got to St. Katherine's he wasn't there, so the police traced his car with the built in GPS. It's police company car, so they can do that. He is here somewhere. I spoke with the police team, insisted they listen to me, told them we have a witness," Bill said, nodding at Robin, "which of course totally freaked them out, but they did pretty quickly fall back into formation, so to speak. They had a few difficult minutes when I tried to convince them that their Chief was the murderer. They had no idea what had happened to him or where he was, because in a murder situation he should be there at St. Katherine's and not have left them. That convinced them to listen to me. They now have men here in the building and searching the grounds." Bill then looked directly at Robin, her face tear streaked, her lips still trembling a bit.

"Yes, sorry, Robin, Chloe is dead. And because of you, we know who did it and that Mark was killed, too. I had a couple of officers stay there to start the search for his body down in all the cavernous basements once the Medical Examiner has arrived to take over supervision of Chloe's body. They will find him. We know Chief Sauder probably still has the knife with him as it was nowhere to be found at the church, and probably he has his service revolver if he thought to wear it to the church tonight. We don't know about that for sure."

There was a noise at the door from the hallway, a pressure against it, but it held firmly against the entry of whomever was trying to get it. The five of them stared in silence, grasping each other, unwilling to believe what was happening here tonight in such an unlikely place on one of the most unlikely of all nights. Then, whomever it was, was gone and it was quiet again.

"Mom!"

"Yes, Robin, it's okay, we are safe in here, "Ann said, hoping it was so. Through the wall, Ann could hear muffled voices next door.

"Oh my, they didn't get Mrs. Ayers moved. I hope, I sure hope this doesn't mean that is where the Chief is right now," Ann said. Bill went to the door, drawing his pistol out of its shoulder holster under his cashmere jacket.

"Everyone stand back, I am going out and I'll check on Mrs. Ayers. If he's there, I'll take him. If not, I'll get her calmed down and locked into her room. John, lock this door behind me as soon as I am out," Bill said. Ann was skeptical. A stranger with a gun in his hand calming down that old woman? That wouldn't calm anyone down.

Bill slipped out, John once again closing and locking the door quickly behind him. As much as they each would have liked to taken charge, saved everyone in the facility, they knew it was currently in the hands of Bill and the couple of local police he had brought with him. Suzanne moved closer to Ann and Robin.

"Oh, Ann, if I had known!" Suzanne said. "And it took me forever to drive here in the snow. Bill had driven to the church and back again in the same amount of time."

"No worries, Suzanne. You could not have known that the Chief of Police of all people was our worst enemy. Who would have guessed that on this Christmas Eve?"

They waited. They couldn't hear much. There was no gun fire, no screams of alarm. Murmurs, yes. Some scuffling. Then quiet. Minutes later a rap of the knuckles on the door, the same gentle rap Ann recognized from all the times at the police station when Bill would gently rap on her open door to announce his presence and not just barge into her space.

"Yes?" John asked quietly.

"It's Bill," he answered. John unlocked and opened the door to let Bill back in.

"Ma'am, it is done. Everything is okay, everyone's all right. Yes, Chief Sauder was in Mrs. Ayers room as you suspected. But he was just sitting there, the knife across his lap, his gun still holstered; silent, waiting like. I think he hadn't yet decided if he would kill the old woman or not, still debating inside of himself if she was enough of a threat to have to kill. But I do think he would have done it once he'd worked up enough courage. Pushing Mark down the stairs in a jealous rage, okay. Slicing Chloe's throat out of anger and power lust, okay, spontaneous and unplanned. But to come and kill an old lady in a hospital bed, I think that was going to take more courage than he came in with. He must have known his time was running out. He knew Robin was here and would have already told us everything she had heard and seen. She was safely with you, and the hunt would be on for him. He'd missed his opportunity to snatch her and get rid of her, sorry ma'am but true, he'd missed it. He knew he'd not get a second chance now.

"He let me walk up to him and take the knife and his gun, and then the other two officers that were in the hallway cuffed him and took him out. He's gone, for good," Bill swallowed hard, finishing his narration. Crime had never been quite so close and so personal for him before this. He figured he'd just blurt it all out and get it over with, all at once. Best for everyone.

John came to Ann and hugged her and Robin, nodding his thanks to Bill and Suzanne. Tomorrow would be better. John said a silent prayer for tomorrow.

Chapter 13

December 25

After the police had left with Chief Sauder, the doctor on duty gave Mrs. Ayers a sedative, took a look at Robin but declared she was fine, just a bit shaken but it would pass. Then with a couple of the nurses, the doctor went room to room to reassure all the patients that all was well, safe and secure again. Things did eventually quiet down. When they did, John suggested he, Robin, Suzanne and Bill go to the farmhouse for some sleep. He would drive all of them in his Jeep. It wasn't far. Tomorrow would be soon enough to deal with it all. By midnight the roads had at least been plowed over once and were moderately okay for the exhausted group to leave Ann so she could get some sleep, and to head to the farmhouse for what was left of the night. Bill promised Suzanne that they would try to get her car out of the Rehab Center parking lot the next day if it wasn't locked behind "Police Line – Do Not Cross" yellow tape. Then she would be able to get back to her house.

When Christmas morning dawned, it was sunny and bright as John had hoped. John and Robin agreed to leave all the presents under the tree untouched until Ann came home. Then they would have a proper Christmas Eve and Christmas Morning, just the three of them. There was still too much to face and deal with today and for the next couple of days. Everyone knew there'd be a lot of time spent with the police recounting the events that led up to last couple of nights and the two murders at St. Katherine's.

Suzanne and Bill had been pointed towards the guest rooms upon arrival. Ann always kept the guest rooms made up, always ready. The guest bath always had a supply of extra things for this very situation – toothbrushes, toothpastes, deodorants, shampoos, soaps, you name it -- in the gaily decorated basket on the back of the toilet. Ann had even had white fluffy robes embroidered with the name of the farm, Mereswood, on them. They hung on the back of the guest room doors. The guest room area was one of the first things that Ann worked on when they had moved in last June, transforming it into a place of welcome for friends and family. When Bill and Suzanne were finally up and dressed, they joined John and Robin in the large country kitchen for coffee and toast.

"I could have done you a quiche," Bill observed. "Yes, next time, I will do a quiche, I promise. I'll get up and have it into the oven early."

"You're quite handy in the kitchen, aren't you?" Suzanne asked.

"Yes, I was blessed with quite a few ladies teaching me the finer things of being a farm woman. I can cook, yes, but you'd be surprised to also know I can mend my own clothes, polish silver, arrange a church tea – well, you get the drift. My dad did his fair share to be sure I could run the tractor, bale hay and shoot a deer in the fall, so don't get me wrong, it wasn't all patent leather and petticoats."

They were able to laugh, and the sound of their laughter surprised them after the seriousness of the last few days. It seemed almost wrong.

"Yes, next Christmas morning, definitely quiche," Bill promised.

When they arrived back at the Rehab Center about ten o'clock, Ann had showered, dressed in her Christmas top that John had been sure to bring to her a few days before, and was waiting in her chair. No physical therapy on Christmas Day she had discovered. The pain medication had allowed her to sleep at least the half of the night that was left to her. She'd knew she'd make up the shortage of sleep over the next several days. This whole Mark – Chloe – Chief Sauder thing had sharpened Ann's resolve to get on with things, face what lay ahead, do the physical therapy, get home and heal completely. And she did have some very interesting news for the foursome this beautiful morning. Bill fetched a few more straight chairs so they could all squeeze in and sit.

"So, what is your news, mom?" Robin asked

"Well, the Buckelsmere Police Department were already here to see me this morning. They did find Mark's body, so they have charged Josh Sauder with two counts of murder. He knows there is a witness, and so has confessed. It looks like it will be an open and shut case. And," Ann paused for dramatic effect, "they have asked me to help out here in Buckelsmere going forward. They are now short a Chief on very short notice, and are understaffed. Since I have moved up here to live, they see it as an opportunity for them and for me. I think it might be just the compromise I need – keep my hand in police work on a consultant basis. I would only be called upon during special, high-end crimes. I wouldn't be working every day in Philadelphia any longer," Ann explained with sparkle in her voice and in her eyes.

"I will wait until after New Year's to give the City notice," she continued and pointed at her hip, "This whole mess falls under worker's comp, so if I leave the Philadelphia Police Force, my coverage is still guaranteed, so that is not a worry. I'll recover up here at home, and start being available to the Buckelsmere Police Department as soon as I am mobile, and driving again."

"Oh, mom," Robin exclaimed, "that is such good news! We'll see so much more of you; it will be so much better!" Ann marveled how the terrors of last night seemed to have faded completely out of Robin's face. Oh, to be young and easy like that again, to be able to heal emotionally so quickly!

"Ann, I'm thrilled, just thrilled. I'll just have to get used to your being around the house, underfoot, so to speak," John added, smiling. Ann knew that John would be very glad to have her around underfoot, that he was really just joking.

"And Suzanne, I am going to take you and your friend, CheChe, up on your offer to teach me how to do family history research. If I can, I will join you in the Daughters of the American Revolution – it would give me something to do other than think about rugs and curtains and such for the farmhouse while I wait for the occasional crime to help solve."

"Fantastic, Ann! We'd love to have you join us. This is great news, and we'd be able to have lunch out, do some shopping . . ." Suzanne rattled on and on.

Ann had left Bill for last. She watched him as Suzanne recited the many things that she and Ann would be able to do together now. She saw that Bill had set his jaw, his facial muscles hard and rigid, trying to smile. She wanted to laugh, but knew that would be unkind. She kept up the pretense of seriousness just a bit longer.

"Bill, that leaves you -- "

"No, ma'am, don't worry about me," Bill interrupted. "We've had three good years. I have learned so much from you. You shouldn't give me a second thought. I am so very pleased for you, especially after all this – the jewelry robberies, the St. Katherine's mess. No, no, don't worry about me. Actually, I've done a lot of thinking and reached a decision myself. I don't want that Philadelphia Police Department life any longer, especially now that I know you will not be going back. I'll finish out these next couple of months, then I'll look for something less demanding, less time consuming and soul sucking because I need to write. There it is. It's true. I feel the need to write, more than anything. That feels good to have admitted out loud. My great aunts have been after me since that story was published a while back, and they want me to follow in their footsteps. So, no, don't worry about me at the Philadelphia Police department. I am so very glad you are moving up and on, rising above this accident," Bill admitted to them.

Ann smiled, "Bill, I was going to ask you to come up here and work with me. The Buckelsmere Police Department was mighty impressed with your investigative skills and then your quick thinking, level headed management of that potentially very explosive situation last night. This morning they are talking about you as if you are divine or something. They want you, too. They will move someone up into the Chief of Police position, and that leaves a spot open. It's only a small little borough in Pennsylvania, nothing much ever happens up here. You might even be bored! There will be lots of time to write, with mental energy left over after the work day to do so. Say yes," Ann asked him.

Bill could not believe what he was hearing. It was Christmas morning, but he'd never believed in the magic of it before. Yes, he'd do it. Why not? How bad could it be? Ann wouldn't be his direct boss, but they would be working together still.

Suzanne, other than offering her opinion that it was absolutely the *best* outcome for all, announced that after their lunch, she was going home to pack and get out of town. She'd had enough distress, death, and destruction. Christmas was here and nothing about it was Christmas. She had decided overnight that although she'd rather go to Rio as it was summer down there, there was that problem of needing a Visa to travel to Brazil. No time for that, so she decided on Vienna. New Year's in Vienna. She'd pull a few strings, call in a few favors, get a good hotel suite, snag a ticket to the Vienna Philharmonic New Year's concert, and be on a plane tomorrow or the next day. She glanced at Bill. Bill glanced at her. Amused, Ann wondered if Bill's passport was in good order. Could it be happening that fast for them?

Suzanne continued, "Yes, and well after that, maybe this summer, maybe I'll throw a lovely house party 'down the shore' as they say in Philly. At my shore house, Diamond Dunes -- oodles of bedrooms and room for everyone. Yes, I say, let's do it. Start making plans for sun and sand and sea, and none of this murder nonsense." Suzanne turned to Ann, "You're so resilient. I wish I could be more like you. Look at you, in here less than a week, making great strides in your recovery *and* you've managed to get yourself a new job! But I'm so completely gutted by the last few days, I simply must get away."

"Oh, no, Suzanne. Just be yourself," Bill said before he realized he had spoken aloud. A blush rose to his cheeks, past the dimples, but he smiled with his eyes, and tried to ignore the momentary lapse of keeping his feelings and thoughts to himself. Awkward, but he would ignore the awkwardness as always.

Christmas dinner came at noon, probably to give as many as possible of the kitchen and wait staff time off for Christmas afternoon and evening. Dinner came on trays for the five of them. The sadness in the room as they all looked at their institutional dinner of turkey slices, potato flake slop, thin gravy, overdone peas was palpable.

Bill looked at it and said, "Next year, I'm cooking a proper dinner."

Before Bill left with Suzanne, both with a Christmas orange and an ironic smile, Bill pulled out a small box from his coat pocket and gave it to Ann. "Just a little something I picked up a few days ago to remember the last few years by. I kinda thought you might not come back to the PPD, that this would be our last Christmas together," he said. She opened it – sterling silver hoop earrings. She laughed. Bill laughed. They all laughed. Ann thought Bill's gift was the perfect reminder of her last case on the Philadelphia Police Department with Bill.

Bill helped Suzanne clean the snow off her car and get it out of the parking space. Suzanne swore she disparately needed to get home and have a double vodka and tonic. Bill watched her drive away, waving a gloved hand in parting to him. Someday soon, Bill told himself and smiled. Yes, someday soon.

John and Robin stayed and watched an old Christmas movie on the TV with Ann who rested in bed. There would be sandwiches and cake in the lobby for supper, with carol singing around the Christmas tree. John and Robin thought they'd give it their best effort, then head home.

Ann felt satisfied that she had decided to leave the city job, the grime and the crime, the troubles there. And finally, alone in bed this Christmas night she felt oddly happy, thankful for John and Robin, Bill and Suzanne. Bill would come to Buckelsmere and they would be able to maintain their professional relationship. John was there for support and love. She didn't know what she'd have done without him these last seven years, and knew the next few years would now be even happier and brighter. Robin was showing signs of growing up, transforming from child to young adult. Ann would look forward to Suzanne's promised beach trip, and also her return to the cottage in Scotland. There would be time before then to decide if it was the right time to talk to Robin about Scotland and Robin's origins. There would be enough time to consider many things. This had been a day of heartbreak for some, as well as a day of renewal for others. Ann was content to let it be.

The world eventually went blue. That time in the winter when the sun sets and everything goes shades of blue before the blackness of night. That rare and special time when the sun sets, the wind stops and that blanket of fresh snow turns indigo and everything is at peace.

Shelly Young Bell

A Proper Christmas Day
Bill Dancer's Menu and Recipes (*Recipes Follow)

Morning
Adaptable to be just Breakfast, or serve a bit later for Brunch
Quiche *
Citrus fruit salad
Broccoli salad *
Bagels / cream cheese
Christmas coffee *
Orange juice

Luncheon
Oyster stew *
Beef vegetable soup *
Oyster crackers

Cocktail Hour
Cheese ball *
Crackers, veggies
Roasted Chestnuts *
Wine

Dinner
Salad Mereswood *
Beef Rib Roast *
    Or Beef Eye Roast *
Yorkshire pudding *
Roasted potatoes, carrots, onion, sprouts *
    Or Mashed Potatoes and Peas
Horseradish sauce *
Rolls, butter
Wine

Cookies, Grandmom's Chocolate Cake *
Coffee

Recipes

Broccoli Salad

2 heads broccoli florets
2/3 cup dried cranberries
1/2 red onion in rings
8 slices bacon, cooked and crumbled.

Dressing:
1 cup mayonnaise
1/2 cup sugar
2 Tablespoons red wine vinegar

Mix first for ingredients, then toss with the dressing. Refrigerate several hours and toss well before serving.

Quiche

3 cups shredded cheddar cheese
1-1/2 cups diced chicken
2/3 cup chopped onion
1 package frozen broccoli, thawed and drained

1-1/3 cups milk
3 eggs
3/4 cup Bisquick
3/4 teaspoon salt if desired
1/4 teaspoon pepper
1/2 teaspoon Italian seasoning

Grease a 10" pie pan. Place chicken, 2 cups of the cheese, onion and broccoli into pie pan. Beat remaining ingredients until smooth. Pour into plate. Bake at 400° 35 minutes or until knife inserted into center comes out clean. Top with remaining cheese. Bake 1-2 minutes until cheese is melted. Serve warm or room temperature.

Soup and Crackers for Lunch?

Yes, soup, because there is so much food coming later today, you will be glad you ate light at lunchtime.

Oyster Stew

For parts of the East Coast, it is NOT Christmas unless there is Oyster Stew. The "purest" recipe does not include the shallot or celery or thyme leaves.
Serves 4-5
1 pint fresh oysters in their liquid
2-1/2 Tablespoons butter
1 large shallot minced very fine
1 stalk celery minced very fine
1 cup heavy cream
2 cups whole milk
½ teaspoon fresh thyme leaves chopped
Salt and pepper to taste.

Set a colander over a small bowl. Add the oysters to the colander, reserving the liquor. Set a fine mesh sieve over another small bowl and pour the oyster liquor into the sieve. This will remove any sand or grit from the liquor. Discard solids.

In a medium saucepan, melt the butter over medium heat. Add the shallots and celery if you are using them, stirring 2-3 minutes until vegetables are slightly softened and translucent.

Turn the heat down to medium low and add the strained oyster liquor, milk, cream and thyme. Heat slowly until broth reaches a simmer (just a few bubbles riming the pan.) DO NOT BOIL, to avoid curdling the milk. Taste the broth and adjust seasoning, adding salt and pepper to taste.

Slip the oysters into the hot broth and let them simmer for 2-3 minutes, just until the edges start to curl. Overcooking will make the oysters rubbery.

Ladle the stew into bowls. Serve with a bowl of Oyster Crackers – "OTC Old Trenton Cracker" Brand if you can find them. Or garnish with celery leaves, Old Bay Seasoning, hot sauce or a pat of butter on top.

Suzanne's Beef Vegetable Soup

Because there is *no way* Suzanne is putting oysters in *her* mouth!

1 Beef Soup Bone
1/2 to 1 lb. additional beef stew meat. Make it as meaty as you'd like.
1-2 Tablespoons oil
4 cups water
1 medium onion, chopped
1 cup cut up celery
1 bag frozen Mixed Vegetables (corn, peas, beans, carrots, lima beans or any combination you want.)

2 cups canned tomatoes diced, slightly mashed to make more tomato sauce for the broth
3 sprigs fresh parsley finely cut
1 Tablespoon salt
1 bay leaf
½ teaspoon freshly ground black pepper.
¼ teaspoon dried marjoram
¼ teaspoon dried thyme

Cut meat off the bone into small pieces. Brown all the meat in the fat in a hot pan. Add water and the bone and simmer 1-1/2 to 2 hours. Remove bone. (Suzanne then refrigerates the stock at this point. The next day, she skims off all the fat from the top and continues with recipe).

Add vegetables, salt, bay leaf, freshly ground pepper, marjoram, and thyme. Cook an additional 20 to 30 minutes until vegetables are tender. Remove bay leaf. Makes 6-8 smallish servings.

You can eliminate the soup bone and water but using prepared low salt beef broth from the grocery store. Just adjust the amount of meat you want in the soup. Suzanne usually doubles the recipe. And it is always better the next day once the flavors have had a chance to mingle with each other.

Pepper Pineapple Cheese Ball

2 - 8 oz packages cream cheese
1/2 cup chopped red and green pepper
2 Tablespoons minced onions
8.5 oz can crushed pineapple, well drained

1 Tablespoon seasoned salt
1/3 cup chopped pecans, to roll the cheese ball in

Bring cheese to room temperature. Mix in all the ingredients except the pecans. Divide and shape into two balls. Roll in the nuts. Serve with crackers, bagel chops, cut vegetables.

Roasted Chestnuts

Buy unblemished glossy chestnuts, bulk, in the produce aisle at your grocery store.
Cut a small cross on one side of each shell.
Place chestnuts in a shallow roasting pan, sprinkle with water.
Roast in 400° F oven for 25-30 minutes.
Wrap hot chestnuts in kitchen towel and squeeze to crush the shells.
Keep nuts wrapped in towel for 5 minutes, then remove hard outer shell and brown skin inside.
Watch you don't burn your fingers!

Salad Mereswood

This salad is plated in the kitchen and set on the dinner plate as you are calling people to the table for dinner.
It is an appetizer and a salad all in one.
Bag of Field Greens
2-3 Large Cooked Shrimp per person, shelled
3 Slices of Cucumber per person
2 Wedges of Tomato per person
Bottled French Dressing.

Place a handful on the Field Greens on the salad plate. Place the cucumber slices on one side of the greens, the tomatoes on the other side, the shrimp up the middle. Drizzle a thin stream of dressing over the top of it all.

Suzanne's One-Sheet Christmas Dinner for Two

Sweet Potatoes, peeled and cubed into ¾" – 1"
Brussel Sprouts, cleaned and halved
Turkey tenderloins, or boneless turkey breast cut down into two portions

Toss vegetables with olive oil, garlic powder, ¼ teaspoon cayenne pepper, ¼ teaspoon paprika, ¼ teaspoon black pepper, 1/8 teaspoon salt.

Toss turkey with olive oil, ¼ teaspoon sage, 1 teaspoon Italian seasoning, ¼ teaspoon salt, ¼ teaspoon black pepper.

Place turkey in middle of greased baking sheet with edges, or large baking dish. Spread the vegetables around the turkey. Drizzle a bit more olive oil on all. Bake at 425° F for 35-40 minutes. Fork test potatoes and veggies for doneness. If you pierce the turkey with a fork, the juice that runs out ought to be clear, NOT pink.

Suggestions: Put some dried cranberries among the veggies for color and a pop of flavor. You can use carrots as well, but microwave them for 3-4 minutes first to be sure they will be cooked and tender.

Want stuffing? Mix some croutons with broth or water, dried sage and green onion and chopped celery. Place in buttered ramekins and bake in hot oven for 20 minutes or until crusty and brown on top.

Use your best crystal and china for a special, easy, 1-hour Christmas dinner! Dessert? Cookies and ice cream!

Perfect Rib Roast

TIMING IS CRITICAL when roasting a rib roast. This recipe will always work but you must
1. Know the weight of the roast
2. Have the roast at room temperature to start with
3. Know the oven is accurate on temperature. Use an oven thermometer to be sure oven temp is exactly 500° F degrees to start with.

You will need to multiply the weight of the roast x 5 minutes per pound. See below. For recipe's purposes I have used 5.5 lb. (about 2 rib bones for 2-4 people).

If you want dinner at a particular time, work backwards so you know when to start the Rib Roast. For example, if dinner is to be served at about 6:30 p.m., put this 5.5 lb. roast into the preheated oven at 3:45 p.m. Turn oven off at 4:13 p.m. Remove from oven at 6:13 p.m. for setting on board, and carving.

5.5 lb. Beef Rib Roast
2 Tablespoons Garlic Powder
2 Tablespoons Onion Powder
1 Tablespoon Black Pepper, freshly ground

Salt
Butter at room temperature

Beef Rib Roast should be at room temperature, so set it out 3-5 hours before roasting.

Preheat oven to 500° F.
Put Beef Rib Roast rib side down in roasting pan. The ribs act as a rack to keep it out of juices.
Rub the roast liberally with the butter.
Sprinkle a generous amount of garlic powder and onion powder over the roast, grind fresh black pepper over the roast. Shake salt over roast. Put roast into the 500° F oven for (5.5 lbs. x 5 minutes per pound = 27.5 then round up) 28 minutes. *Adjust this time to the weight of your roast.* At the end of the time you have calculated, TURN THE OVEN OFF, DO NOT OPEN THE OVEN DOOR, WALK AWAY FOR 2 HOURS. Roast will be MEDIUM RARE, with the ends being a bit more done.
After 2 hours, remove the roast to carving board, slice and serve. If your slice the meat off the bones first, you can then more easily slice it into 4 generous servings. Save the bones for another recipe. Serve with au jus from the pan, and horseradish sauce.

Perfect Eye Roast of Beef
Sometimes it is easier and more economical to do an Eye Roast.

4 lb. Eye Round Roast
Salt
Pepper
Olive oil
4 garlic cloves, smashed

1 yellow onion, thickly sliced
4 sprigs fresh Rosemary

Season roast with salt and pepper and refrigerate overnight. Remove from refrigerator 2 hours before roasting. Preheat oven to 400° F. Rub roast with olive oil and coat roasting pan with olive oil. Add the garlic and onion slices and rosemary to the bottom of the pan, place roast on top of them. Cook for 30 minutes, then baste. Reduce to 350° F and cook until meat registers medium-rare (internal temp of 125-130*F), about 1 hour and 15 minutes. *Test the roast after 45 minutes so you catch it before it overcooks, just in case!* Remove from oven when 125-130° F internal temperature, place on craving board, uncovered for 20 minutes. Slice roast and serve. I put a pan of prepared root veggies and quartered red potatoes into the oven at the same time, removing them when they are cooked and tender, about an hour.

Bill's Signature Horseradish Sauce

1 cup sour cream
salt and pepper, to taste
2 Tablespoons prepared horseradish
1 teaspoon Dijon mustard
1 teaspoon white wine vinegar

Mix together, adjust seasonings to taste, refrigerate for up to one day.

Yorkshire Pudding

Preheat oven to 450° F. Grease the pans and *preheat the pan*.
Put into bowl:
2 eggs
Beat them until they are light, then add
1 cup milk
1 tablespoon melted butter
1 cup all-purpose flour
1/4 teaspoon salt

Beat the mixture until thoroughly blended, 30 seconds. The batter should have the consistency of heavy cream. Add more milk if necessary. Put a teaspoon of meat drippings in each pan if you have meat drippings. *Put the mixture into preheated greased pans. Do not skip this step.* Fill pans about half full. Bake 20 minutes, then reduce heat to 350° F. Bake another 20 minutes. Then test one to be sure they are fished. This is important because often the Yorkshire puddings appear fully baked when they are not actually finished.

Roasted potatoes, baby carrots, onion, sprouts

Precook baby carrots in microwave or stovetop for 3-4 minutes before roasting.
Cut red potatoes and onions into quarters.
Toss potatoes, onion, baby carrots and cleaned Brussel sprouts in olive oil until coated.
Sprinkle lightly with garlic powder, salt, pepper and parsley flakes.
Roast at 400° F on greased baking pan for 40-50 minutes, until fork tender. If cooking with something else in the oven (not the Rib Roast!) you might need to adjust the time if oven is set lower or higher.

Mashed Potatoes and Peas

Peel and boil 5 lbs. of white potatoes until fork tender. Drain. Mash by hand or with mixer with ½ cup milk or cream, and ½ stick butter, salt and pepper to taste. Do not over mix if using electric mixer as the potatoes will become gluey.

Use Frozen Peas and cook as package suggest. Drain, toss with butter and a dash of salt and pepper.

Irish Oatmeal Cookies

Mix together:
1/2 cup softened butter
1/4 cup firmly packed dark brown sugar
1/4 cup white granulated sugar
1/2 egg slightly beaten
1/2 teaspoon vanilla extract
1/2 teaspoon baking soda
1/2 teaspoon salt
1/2 teaspoon cinnamon
Stir in
3/4 cup all-purpose flour
1-1/2 cups McCann's Quick Cooking Irish Oatmeal. This oatmeal makes melt-in-your-mouth cookies.
1/8 cup dried cranberries or raisins
1/4 cup chopped walnuts or pecans

Drop by rounded teaspoons onto ungreased cookie sheet. Bake for 12-13 minutes at 350° F. Cool for one minute before removing to wire rack.

Butter Cookie Cut-Outs

1 cup butter softened
1 cup sugar
1 egg
2-1/2 cups all-purpose flour
1 teaspoon baking powder
2 Tablespoons orange juice
1 teaspoon vanilla

Combine butter, sugar and egg. Beat until light and fluffy. Stir in rest of ingredients until well combined. Chill 2-3 hours. Preheat oven to 400° F. Cut dough in half, and roll out on floured board to 1/4" to 1/2 ". Cut with cookie cutters. Bake on ungreased cookie sheet for 10 minutes or until golden brown on edges. Cool on wire rack. Frost or decorate as desired.

Butter Frosting
Mix 3 cups confectioner's sugar with 1/3 cup softened butter, 1-2 Tablespoons milk and 1 teaspoon vanilla. Beat on high for 1-2 minutes. Ice completely cooled cookies, then decorate as you like.

Coconut Macaroons

1-1/3 cups coconut
1/3 cup sugar
3 Tablespoons flour
1/8 teaspoon salt
2 egg whites
1/2 teaspoon almond extract
Candied cherry halves

Combine all but the Cherry Halves together. Drop by teaspoons onto lightly greased cookie sheet. Press a cherry half onto the top of each cookie. Bake at 325° F for 20-25 minutes or until edges are golden brown. Remove from cookie sheet immediately.

Snowballs or Italian Wedding Cookies

1 cup butter (do not substitute)
1/2 cup sifted powdered sugar
1 teaspoon vanilla
2 cups all-purpose flour
1 cup chopped walnuts or pecans
Sifted powdered sugar

Beat butter on high for 30 seconds. Beat in the 1/2 cup powdered sugar and vanilla until combined. Beat in as much flour as you can, then mix the rest of the flour and nuts by hand. Roll into 1" balls. Place 2" apart on u greased cookie sheet. Bake 350° F for 18-20 minutes until lightly browned. Transfer to cooling rack. Roll cooled cookies in sifted powdered sugar.

Mrs. Dancer's Molasses Sugar Cookies

1/4 cup shortening, melted
1 cup white sugar
1/4 cup molasses
1 egg
Beat the above ingredients together.
Add the following to the wet mixture and mix completely:

2 teaspoons baking soda
2 cups flour
1/2 teaspoon cloves
1/2 teaspoon dried ground ginger
1 teaspoon cinnamon
1/2 teaspoon salt
Chill the dough. Form into 1" balls, roll in granulated sugar. Place 2" apart on greased cookie sheet. Press cookie tops down with fork.
Bake 375° F for 8-10 minutes.

Suzanne's Orange Walnut Date Bars
Because these are one of John's Favorites

1 cup all-purpose flour
½ teaspoon baking soda
½ teaspoon cinnamon
¼ teaspoon salt
¼ teaspoon nutmeg
1/3 cup softened butter
¾ cup brown sugar
1 egg
1 Tablespoon orange zest
2 Tablespoons orange juice
½ cup chopped dates
¾ cup chopped walnuts

Preheat oven to 350° F. Grease and flour 11" x 7" pan. Sift together first 5 ingredients in a medium bowl. In a larger bowl, beat together butter and sugar. Add egg, orange zest and orange juice. Add flour mixture, dates and walnuts. Pour into pan. Bake at 350° F for 25-30 minutes. Let cool in pan. Ice when completely cool.

Icing

¼ cup softened butter
1 teaspoon orange zest
1 egg yolk
1 teaspoon vanilla
2 cup sifted powdered sugar
2 Tablespoons orange juice

Beat all ingredients together in small bowl until combined. Do not ice bars until the day before or day of use or they will get yucky.

Grandmom's Chocolate Cake
It's Christmas and Some of Us Want Chocolate!

Stir together with large slotted spoon:
1-1/2 cup flour
1 cup sugar
1 teaspoon baking soda
1/2 teaspoon salt
3 Tablespoons cocoa

Add to the above dry mixture and mix:
5 Tablespoons shortening or cooking oil
1 Tablespoon cider vinegar
1 cup water
1 teaspoon vanilla

Pour into greased and floured 8-9" cake pan. Bake at 350° F for 35 minutes. Ice as desired. A nice white buttercream allows you to decorate with colored sugars or sprinkles for Christmas.

Beverages

Christmas Coffee. Bill puts a teaspoon of ground cinnamon in with the ground coffee in the coffee maker basket before brewing. Obviously in this day of pod coffee, you can buy a Christmas blend. Bill's dad serves his Christmas morning coffee using unflavored French Roast black coffee, with a dash of anise-flavored liqueur in the cup once brewed.

Wine. It's Christmas, have white, red, and a sparkling Italian wine available from brunch on! Don't buy the cheapest you can find, but there is no need to buy the most expensive ones either. You will be able to get *very* drinkable wines for between $10 and $15 each bottle.

Non-Alcoholic. Bill always has bottles of spring water, and Italian sparkling water available as well. He is not a soda drinker, but don't forget soda for your quests. Iced Tea and Lemonade are nice non-alcoholic alternatives.

Shelly Young Bell worked in industry as an Art Director and Director of Communications while also pursuing her writing. Most recently, she is the author of *The Phoenix Mysteries,* a series of novellas and short stories set near her home in Doylestown, PA. and *Stand Like the Brave*, a Historic Fiction book about a shell-shocked WW1 vet facing WW2.

Facebook: Shelly Young Bell, Mystery Writer
https://www.facebook.com/pg/ShellyYoungBell/

Books by Shelly Young Bell

The Phoenix Detective Mysteries
A Very Sisterly Murder, Book 1
Murder at St. Katherine's, Book 2
The Diamond Dunes Murders, Book 3
The Cabot College Murders, Book 4
Population 10, The Dead End Murders, Book 5
R.S.V.P. to Murder, Book 6
Murder on the Promenade Deck, Book 7
Murder at 13 Curves, Book 8

Historic Novel
Stand Like the Brave

All available on Amazon under Shelly Young Bell

Made in the USA
Middletown, DE
13 November 2023

42609820R00083